Mal de Ojo

(Book 2: Life of
Elias Butler)

D. C. Adkisson

This book is a work of fiction. Names, places, characters and incidents are a work of the author's imagination or are used fictionally. Any resemblance or reference to any actual locales, events or persons, living or dead is entirely fictional. However, as far as the author has studied the traits of the individual are true to the characters.

Cover photograph of Rio Grande by D.C. Adkisson.

DEDICATION

Throughout life many people cross our trails. Some are unnoticed, others become acquaintances, those we may call friends. But then there are those who are there for you in the storms and tough situations in life. There most likely will only be a handful or two of these types of people—true friends. To those "friends" this book is dedicated!

CONTENTS

ACKNOWLEDGMENTS

I would like to give personal thanks to Janet Kessler and Perla Loftin for helping me with the Spanish. Any mistakes are either intentional for the book, or are my own.

Again I must give special credit to my wife. She was my critic, my editor, my antagonist and my encourager in the writing of my second novel. She definitely put in a labor of love to help me. Special thanks to my daughter Kimberly who was a great help in the proofing of the book.

I have wondered if recognition of the Lord belonged in the dedication or here. I give Him honor and praise for in everything there should be proper acknowledgment of Him.

Prologue

I saw them drive up and park. Jason was driving; he is the husband of my sister, Betsy. Also in the car was my brother Will. They are coming for blood, my blood. Actually, they are coming for money; all they seem to care about is money. What a shame!

Several months ago I had discovered an old trunk while cleaning the barn. I was supposed to get it cleaned out so we could sell the place. In the process I found a treasure hidden in that trunk; it was full of bits and pieces of the life of my great grandfather, Elias Butler.

In that trunk there were two pistols and a shotgun plus several badges. There were all kinds of clippings and partial clippings from newspapers and several journals. I had become fascinated when I began to read the journals; it seemed as if I could actually feel a pulse.

It had been a chore sorting them out; some of the pages were torn, some yellowed beyond reading, and some of the journals and articles were not dated. My great grandpa had gone up the cattle trail from Texas to Abilene, Kansas, and after returning to Texas, it seems that he started to work for McNelly's Rangers.

There came the knock at the door, and they entered

before I could get there to open it. The first words from Betsy's mouth, "When do we get our money?"   I was polite, or tried to be. "Good to see you too, Sis."

They came on into the living room, declining the coffee I offered. When a person does that, a warning flag goes up in my mind. Who turns down a cup of coffee?

I began to explain the situation. As soon as I could sell my place I'd buy them out. I assured them they would get their money, but needed to be patient. Again I tried to tell them about what I found, except for the money that was in the trunk. I figured they didn't need to know that, at least for now.

Jason wanted to see the guns, but Betsy grabbed him and said it was time to go. They'd been here, oh, maybe all of twenty minutes. Guess they just wanted to make their demands in person.

After they left I went back to the second journal. Inside was an article. The article was torn, and what I could make out from the heading was, "Evil...Ashes."

Chapter 1 – The Call to Austin

I hated the thought of going to Austin. That place seemed to be the hot seat of politics. Politics, that is a word to rile up the innards. Myself, just let me ride the range and do my job, but because of the politics it was becoming harder to do the job.

Perhaps if old Abe Lincoln had not been shot, Texas would not be in this mess. But we must live life as it is; try to live according to the Lord's commands, and don't dwell on the "ifs" that come. But these Carpetbaggers sure make the going rough sometimes.

Now don't get me wrong. I'm not of the notion that all those folk from the North are evil men. Some are surely good, Jim Constance for one, my pal Miles Forrest is another, and I've read of what General Howard had tried to do. However, there are a flood of them in the government, and it is clearly seen among our group, the State Police.

I was fortunate to be serving under Captain McNelly. People sure have attacked him for working with the State Police. He just rubs at his goatee, smiles, and in that calm manner of his would say, "If something is evil, then it is the duty of good men to stand firm and try to correct the situation."

He's right, of course, but that don't make it any easier, and sometimes evil corrupts the good. Miles and I have often discussed this. Both of us have come to the conclusion that the primary reason men are evil is greed. If man could control his greed, the world would be a better place. What was that last commandment, "Thou shalt not covet"?

McNelly called several of us to meet him in Austin. Hidalgo rode in with me. We had been checking some problems over by San Angelo. He and I worked well together; I made the coffee, but he did the cooking. Now, I consider myself a fair cook having had a good teacher in Jackson, but there's something that Mexican does to food that makes it a real delight. However, I do prefer biscuits to those flat little pieces he calls "*tortillas*".

His full name is Benito Hidalgo, but all I've ever heard him called was Hidalgo. Now, I'm not a big man, maybe that's why I like him. He couldn't be more than 5'6" and thin, but that's all tough gristle. But I was also jealous; he sports a full black mustache. I've been working on mine, but it's a sore sight compared to his.

He was not only a good cook, but he proved to be a hard worker. He was good with a gun and also with that knife he carried. You never had to tell him to do something; he was already doing it. Yep, a good man to have with you on the trail.

We were up near San Angelo, just finishing up a job, when the news came to us that we were to come to Austin. We were to be there the middle of next month, so hopefully we could finish up our business here. There was a need for cattle ever since Goodnight began that drive. In fact, the trail I rode to Abilene was now becoming known as the Chisholm Trail. Folks back East wanted steak and

Texas had plenty to provide.

It seemed it was easier for this one gang to let ranchers round up cattle, then they would come and rustle them. They only picked on small ranchers, realizing the larger ones had the men to come after them. The army at Fort Concho couldn't deal with it as there were still plenty of problems with the Comanches. Therefore, Hidalgo, myself, and Ty Albright were sent up to investigate.

This country was still all open range and unbranded cattle belonged to whomever could rope it and slap a brand on it. The larger outfits swung a wide loop, but were tolerant of the small ones as long as they didn't begin to brand unweaned calves.

These small ranchers usually did all the work themselves; rarely did they have cowboys working for them. If they did, it would be only one or two punchers. Because of that they couldn't go trail the rustlers.

That outlaw pack must have had a leader with a head on his shoulders. If there were two hundred head of cattle, they would only steal fifty-sixty head at a time. The ranchers had to stay with the rest of the herd.

We stopped at the ranch of Pete Michaels. He was the one who sent for the investigation. I said ranch, but it was only a wooden shack; barely enough to keep the cold wind and rain out. It was kept up, however, and had a small barn and corral.

Riding up to the house, we stayed mounted and helloed the house. Shortly a woman came out with a shotgun pointed our direction. The toil of living on the Texas frontier was already showing on her face. There were lines of tension and worry drawn on her forehead and the beginning of crow's feet around her eyes. The flour dusting her apron indicated she might have something baking in the oven. Peeking from the doorway was a youngster; maybe four years old or so.

I tipped my hat. "Howdy ma'am, we were contacted by Mr. Michaels to investigate some rustlin'. My name's Elias Butler; these other two men are Benito Hidalgo and Ty Albright," I hesitated. "Is Mr. Michaels hereabouts?"

She hadn't lowered the shotgun, a good sign that she wasn't going to trust the three strangers that had just arrived at her door. "Should be here before supper," she said curtly.

I shifted my eyes to the youngster that had come from his hiding place in the shack. She must have noticed, for she turned. "Peter! Get back in the house!" Then whirled facing us again.

"Mrs. Michaels, we don't want to bother you." I looked around. "Any place we can water our horses?"

"Over there; there's a stream."

"Thank you ma'am. We'll wait there until your husband returns. Oh, and Mrs. Michaels, don't turn your head away when you have men in front of you. They may not be friendly like us."

CHAPTER 2 – Meeting with Pete Michaels

We stayed at the stream for close to an hour just lounging around, waiting for Michaels to return. It was about twenty yards from the house, and there were a few cottonwoods for shade. Ty and Hidalgo picked up some sticks for a fire and I dug out the old coffeepot and coffee. Seems like I've had that pot forever, but really only a few years now.

We sat back, talked a little, and drank coffee. It wasn't long before we heard Hidalgo snoring. Mercy, that guy can go to sleep faster than anyone I've known. He told me once that it was from a pure, clean conscious, plus the fact that his father told him when on the trail to get sleep while the getting was good.

Time drifted by slowly, at least for Ty and I, but we had no place to go in a hurry. It was an hour or so that a man rode up to the corral and dismounted. We reckoned that was Pete Michaels. I kicked Hidalgo's boot to waken him. We tightened our cinches, mounted and rode on down.

He had unsaddled his horse, put him in the corral, and was putting some hay in the manger when we approached. He looked up, and I noticed he started for his saddle. His rifle was in the scabbard. He should have had that rifle with him, in case there had been trouble around.

I wanted to put him at ease. "Mr. Michaels, we have been sent from Austin to check out the situation." I hesitated to use the name State Police as they were some who didn't take kindly to that name.

He came over and shook everyone's hand as I introduced us. "Come on up to the house. I'm sure the Missus has enough for supper."

"You sure?" asked Ty.

Michaels glared at Ty. "I wouldn't have asked if we didn't! We may not be rich as some, but we are neighborly and won't turn anyone away hungry."

As we were walking to the house he said, "Not much room inside, so get your plate an' come back out on the porch."

It wasn't long before we had a plate of pintos and ham. It may not be my favorite meal, but it's one I can eat most any day. We each had a biscuit, and as we sat down Mrs. Michaels came out with the coffee pot.

"Hope you don't mind coffee as we're out of buttermilk."

Michaels began to give us the run down on events. Personally he had lost sixty head, and only had thirty-five or so left for market. He remarked that he didn't know if he could hold out the year.

"Know where they take them?" I asked.

"No. We've trailed them to the east so might be Fort Worth. But a couple of times we trailed them west, so maybe Mexico."

"When was the last time they hit?" questioned Ty.

"Three, maybe four weeks ago. The Ryder crew is ready to head north the next couple days so this would be a good time for them to hit again," he paused. "This would for sure do me in."

We hashed around some thoughts. It was decided that I would work with the crew while Benito and Ty sort of hung around, staying out of sight.

As we were getting up to go, Michaels offered for us to stay in his barn. We declined.

I noticed Hidalgo rummaging through his bags and lifted a bag of what I supposed was coffee. Michaels had already gone back into the house, so Hidalgo set it on the back of the chair. Most likely we had finished most of the coffee they had left.

CHAPTER 3 – Rustlers

The next evening I was riding the first shift of night guard. We had decided that I would join the crew. If three new hands showed up the rustlers might get suspicious if they had someone watching. Ty and Hidalgo would separate to each side of the herd and stay out of sight.

Riding around the herd I thought that the attack had to come tonight. The small herd would merge with the larger one day after tomorrow, so tomorrow night would be cutting it too close.

Looking up I noticed the moon. It was just a sliver in the sky. It was going to be a dark night; a night perfect for rustlers to show up.

There were three of us, each riding three hour shifts. The two hundred head of cattle were restless, not being used to each other as there were five smaller outfits that had merged. They would graze, then shuffle around; restless as if they expected something to happen. This would stop once they had spent a few days on the trail.

A fellow named Billy Johnson came out to relieve me, but I didn't ride back to camp. There was a little draw that I rode into and moved back into the shadows. This was a perfect night; it was dark, the cattle were restless, the raid had to come tonight.

I didn't dare relax, but the night drew on and the silence grew louder. It had to have been close to an hour later that I finally eased back in my saddle. Now, don't things seem to work that way? As soon as I relaxed I heard horses moving up the same draw where I was situated. If I had relaxed an hour ago they might have shown up then.

I tried to move deeper in the draw, speaking softly to Fred so he wouldn't snort as the other horses approached. We were upwind, so hopefully their horses wouldn't smell Fred.

They were just thirty yards from me when they moved out of the draw toward the herd. As they passed I counted seven. Then I heard shots from the far side of the herd. The cattle started to rush in my direction and the rest of the gang was there on the side to pick off fifty-seventy head.

The rustlers were waiting for the herd to get close and for the leaders to go on by before they went into action. I saw one lift a rifle and fire. There were only silhouettes but I could see a rider fall right after the shot. Now it was chaos; shooting, the rush of the cattle; it was time for me to get involved.

From the south came a man, riding hard, and firing. It had to be Ty, and his shooting had an affect as I saw one rustler fall. They returned fire and Ty's horse went down.

"Yeehaw, Fred! Let's go!"

The rustlers had been too intent on the herd and not expecting us to be waiting for them. There were shots in the distance; I reckoned that was Hidalgo. There were at least two rustlers down and the herd had turned to the West at a trot. It seemed they were slowly turning back toward their original graze.

I fired again at a darkened figure. They halted and all

began shooting at my position. About that time Hidalgo rode up shooting back at them. Being grouped together they made better targets. There must have been a mite of good sense among them for they left off trying to get the herd and skedaddled out of there with only half their number.

I spurred my horse to the spot where I saw Ty drop. I found him lying there, not moving, beside his downed horse. Dismounting I moved toward him. It was too dark to see much, but I felt for a pulse and found him alive. Checking him over the best I could and didn't detect any blood loss.

When I tried to move him, he groaned. Grabbing his arm his eyes opened and he moaned. "Don't, think it's broke." At least now he was conscious.

He reached up and touched his head. "Must of hit it when muh hoss went down."

While I was checking Ty a shrill whistle sounded. "Hidalgo," I said. "Stay here, Ty."

"My hoss is dead, and I don't feel much like walkin' so where do yuh think I'd go?"

Mounting I rode toward the sound. I couldn't see any movement, but then I heard the whistle again, just off to my left. Hidalgo must have heard me approach.

"Elias, we have one partially alive."

"Build us a little fire. I'd like to see what he looks like."

"I see you," came a snarl. "I see you through the eyes of *el Diablo*. I look into your soul. It is now worthless and will soon die."

Looking at Hidalgo who now had a little fire started, "Diablo?"

"The devil," remarked Hidalgo. "The man is loco— crazy."

"You think I'm loco? Diablo is looking at you now. He will have your lives."

"Where were you plannin' on takin' the cattle?"

"He is calling; soon you will see," the man groaned. "He will give you both a slow, painful death. You will see, he is bringing your worthless souls to him."

"Sorry, you're wrong there. This soul was given over to Jesus Christ many years back."

When I said that, there came a sound that would cause your gizzard to shudder. It was a mixture of a snarl and the howl of a wounded wolf. I looked at Hidalgo whose eyes were wide and shone in the firelight, and then back to the man who uttered that frightful sound. He was dead.

CHAPTER 4 – Thoughts in the Night

"Hello, the fire!" came the voice of a rider. There were three mounted men moving slowly our direction. I recognized the voice of a man called "Brick."

"Come on in," I yelled. As they rode to the light of the fire I noticed one man slumped over in his saddle.

"Peter caught a bullet," said Brick. "There's quite a bit of blood and I can't see much, too dark."

"Should we stay here, or go back to camp?" asked the other rider.

"I don't think we should move Pete until we can get a better look at the damage. Caleb, you go on back and let the others know the situation. We'll stay here for the night."

Hidalgo was already helping Michaels down so I went to help. He was conscious and groaned a mite. We laid him down by the fire. "We saved your herd, Mr. Michaels," I said. Then I grabbed the legs of the dead man and drug him out of camp.

I muttered to no one in particular. "Not goin' to let this vermin lie next to a good man."

These were good men. As soon as Michaels was

settled and as comfortable as we could make him, Hidalgo went to his tote bag and started water to boiling for coffee and to clean up Michaels some. Brick was out scrounging for more wood. Yes, these were good men; they didn't have to be told what to do around camp.

I went over and mounted Fred. "Goin' to go get Ty." I was hoping I could find him again in the dark. Hoping he was awake and would let out a yell when I was close.

I rode to where I though I left him, but he wasn't around and neither was the dead horse. It was almighty dark and there were still a few hours before gray light would come around. I didn't think I was off that much. Looking back I could see our little fire glowing in the night.

Then I remembered veering just off to the left and up on a hillside. Maybe I just hadn't gone far enough. Riding on a few yards further and moving slightly to the right I thought I saw a shape on the ground.

"Could be a dead horse," I mumbled to myself or maybe to Fred.

We moved closer and then heard a voice, just above a whisper. "Butler, that you?"

"Ty, where are you? I can't see a thing."

"Almost ten yards off your right shoulder," he paused. "I'll try to stand."

Moving slowly to the right I thought I saw some movement. Then I saw him, as he slumped back to the ground.

"Pretty woozy, Elias. I saw the fire and started crawlin' that way. Tried to stand, but everything starts to whirl."

"Let's get you on over there." I reached down to help him up.

"Careful, the arm!"

Between his arm and his dizziness it took a few

minutes to get him mounted. As I mounted behind him Fred turned his head as if to bite one of us.

"Don't you dare! Bite me and you can lay over there with your dead cousin. You can for sure carry the two of us that distance."

He snorted as if to say, "but I don't have to like it."

Arriving back at our camp there was little to do but wait out the night. Michaels was asleep; I noticed that he was cleaned up and bandaged, probably Hidalgo.

"He is a lucky man," said Hidalgo. "Bullet just grazed his side right along his ribcage. There's lots of blood, and he should be sore a few days, but unless infection sets in, there should be no problem."

The two of us got Ty off the horse. Hidalgo checked him over. He wasn't shot, just a cut and knot on his head, and a broken arm for which Hidalgo quickly rigged up a sling.

We sat there, drank some coffee, and counted our blessings. No one was dead; Pete had lost some blood, but it was a graze. We didn't know of anyone else being hurt and there was no shooting from the far side after the attack started. The herd was safe, but we wouldn't know until morning if any beeves were missing. I didn't think so, but if there were they would be in the area. One more day and the herd would be moving north; that little outlaw band, hurt as bad as they were, would not be trying to attack again.

The night was still; as it normally does just before gray light appears, it turned cooler. Sure was glad Brick had scrounged up more wood.

"How're they doin'?" asked Brick.

"Well, they're sleepin' peaceful." Then there came a sound not far from us.

A little laugh came from Brick. "How 'bout him?"

"Brick, all I can tell you is that he must have a pure heart. He can go to sleep anywhere and do it immediately." I looked over at Hidalgo. "He does tend to make some noise though."

Brick held his cup over and I poured him some coffee. "One good thing; when we're on the trail and there may be danger lurkin', he doesn't snore a lick. But tonight, well, just take a listen."

"Think we should set up a guard?" asked Brick.

"Probably don't need to, but it wouldn't be wise not to. You go ahead and get some sleep, I'm still too wired. I'll wake you in a couple of hours."

He went back to his horse, unsaddled it, then pulled his bedroll off and came back to the fire.

I poured myself another cup of coffee and sat there musing over the day and those strange words from the dead bandit. I sure wasn't going to fret none over what he said. However, the thought of the devil seeing me was none too comfortable.

"Lord," I began to whisper a prayer. "Was that jasper just runnin' his mouth or is there something that I should be worryin' about? But I do want to be thankin' You for Your protectin' hand tonight...on all of us."

I kept my eyes moving round the outside of the camp. It was still dark and I figured it was three hours before dawn. Then I felt an answer in my soul. "Never worry--trust Me."

CHAPTER 5 – Fort Concho

The next morning we accessed our losses. Only Ty and Michaels had been hurt and only four head of cows were missing from the herd.

Ty tried to ride the next day but each step of his horse jostled his arm causing him to groan. Hidalgo had his arm tightly bound, but it didn't seem to help; however, he was able to make it the few miles to Michael's house.

Michael's wife was alarmed. The ride had opened up Pete's wound and blood seeped through his shirt. She hurried him to the house, not giving us a second look. Guess she took care of him there.

Hidalgo and I figured we needed to get Ty to a doctor. Borrowing Michael's wagon, we loaded it with hay giving Ty a more comfortable place to lay. Hopefully that would keep him from being jostled too much. We were about ten miles from Fort Concho.

It took most of the day and, thank goodness, Ty slept most of the way. His groaning was getting to me. We stopped once for coffee and to give the mules a breathing spell.

Fort Concho, one of the many forts along the Texas

frontier was built upon the banks of the Concho River with its purpose to protect the frontier settlements. Arriving at the fort the corporal of the guard directed us to the largest structure on the fort—the hospital.

I went on in to find a doctor. They actually had a couple at the fort. The one I talked to was a tall man, with reddish hair and goatee that was finely trimmed. He quickly ordered the soldiers out and one grabbed a litter on the way.

After placing Ty on the stretcher they took him inside. Hildalgo and I started to go with Ty into this little room, but the doc shooed us out. We stood outside and from time to time we would hear Ty moan and a couple of times give out a yell. I looked at Hildalgo and nodded; we agreed it was best for us to stay out. Thirty, maybe forty minutes later the doc came out along with another guy helping Ty.

"He can't be traveling for a while. His forearm and clavicle are broken" the doctor informed us.

"Clavicle?" I questioned. "What's a clavicle?"

"Collar bone," he replied, pointing out the bone below and to the left of my neck.

"Nothing much we can do about it except bandage him tightly and make sure he doesn't move much. Not sure of the forearm. I don't think it's a compound fracture, but it needs to be completely stable; I don't want the bone to move and cut an artery or vein.

I looked at Hidalgo, and then back to the doc. "So what are you sayin'?"

"No movement; bed rest for at least four weeks."

"He's supposed to be in Austin, just shy of two weeks."

"Well, he won't make it. Too dangerous in case the break is compound. Plus that collar bone won't heal properly either." He turned and looked at Ty who seemed to be showing the strain and pain was etched ot the corner of his mouth. He was very pale.

Turning back to us the doc said, "And the trip would be very painful."

Ty looked at us and shook his head. The doctor nodded at the orderly who then took Ty into another room filled with beds. "We'll see to him. Don't worry, just explain the situation to your boss."

There wasn't much we could do. Thanking the doctor we shook his hand and took our leave. We stopped by to tell Ty goodbye, told him to rest easy and that McNelly would understand.

We stopped at the sutler's before leaving the fort. As I was picking up some necessities for the ride, such as coffee, beans, bacon, and flour, Hildalgo nudged me. He didn't have to say anything; we more than doubled the order.

"You're right," I said. "I should have thought of it. The Michaels could do with some extra food. We need to take the wagon back and should check on him before we leave anyhow."

When we got to the ranch Pete was sitting out on the porch. He stood up as we approached, slowly I might add. I took the wagon over by the corral and turned the mules loose. Hidalgo, without dismounting, leaned over and dropped a couple of pokes on the porch.

"Thought you could use this," he said.

Before Michaels could object I interjected, "How're you feelin'?"

I filled him in on Ty's condition. "When I get back on my feet I'll go visit him," he replied. He seemed tired; he must have lost more blood than we first thought.

I mounted up. "See you next time through, Pete." He

waved and we returned it and rode out. I happened to glance toward the barn and Mrs. Michaels was standing just inside the doorway. Even from the distance I could make out her scowl.

CHAPTER 6 – On the Trail to Austin

Riding with Hidalgo alongside was enjoyable. There was no wasted talk or action and I didn't cotton to much talk on the trail. Oh, I might say a few words to Fred from time to time, but I preferred the solitude of the ride.

We figured on 8-10 days to reach Austin riding through some of the most beautiful country in Texas. Topping a hill to look out over the vista was a magnificent sight with the hills and slopes. The streams were all spring fed; that's good water.

It was the second night out and Hidalgo's turn to cook. "Say, amigo, fix up some of those round, flat pieces of bread—those tortillas."

Elias, they're pronounced *tor tee yas.*"

"Spelled tortillas, but no matter, they're almost as good as biscuits."

"Aye, my friend, will you never learn any of my language?"

"What do you mean? I called you 'amigo'."

He laughed and went to work. I went out and gathered up wood for the fire. After getting a good supply

I went down to the stream to fill up the coffeepot.

There was a breeze making the evening nice and peaceful. Hildalgo filled those tortillas with fried bacon and beans prepared with just a dash or two of chili powder that he always carried. That along with a pot of coffee satisfied our stomachs.

Darkness was just settling in and we were finishing up the coffee.

"Is it true?" he asked.

"Is what true?"

"What you told Stiles back in Abilene?"

Goodness, I thought, that was a few years ago. "Where'd that come from?" I asked.

"Been thinking on it." he paused. "I was raised to believe, but it wasn't as simple as you put it. Most of us Mexicans are Catholic."

"Benito, it is that simple. Just believe in Jesus."

It was quiet after that. He put another couple of pieces of wood on the fire and went to lay on his bedroll. I set my cup on a rock and he did the same. No more words were spoken, there was only the sounds of the night, in the distance the cry of the lonely coyote.

On the fifth day out we stopped at the Fulcher homestead. They had a nice plot of land and cabin along Brady Creek. As was typical of most on the frontier, they were anxious for news.

Sitting at the supper table we told of what took place up at San Angelo. In return we feasted on ham, grits, cornbread, and pintos. Another custom on the frontier; always feed your guests.

"If I'd know you were coming I'd have made a fig pie," remarked Nancy Fulcher. "Stay over a day and I'll bake one."

Hildalgo and I looked at each other. "Temptin'

ma'am," I replied. "But we best not." And I meant that it was tempting; it had been quite a while since either of us had a piece of pie.

We finished the coffee and rose from the table. "Gracias," said Hidalgo.

"Mrs. Fulcher, thank you. I haven't eaten that good in quite a spell."

I turned my head and looked at Mr. Fulcher. "Alright if we bunk in the barn?"

"That'd be fine. Sorry, we don't have any spare rooms. By the way, the name's Henry."

We turned to leave. "We expect you for breakfast."

"Eggs, biscuits 'n' gravy, grits," joined in Mrs. Fulcher with a smile. "And I still have some jam I haven't opened."

I looked at Hidalgo and he smiled. "It will be a treat. We will be here."

We spent another four days on the trail. After leaving the Fulcher's we traveled east to the Colorado River and then followed the river on down to Austin.

I was usually up first to put the coffee on and read from my Bible. Since the time I rode with Stiles I also spent some time acquainting my hand with my gun. Some folk scoff at ritual, but these were two I tried to practice everyday without fail. Either one of them could save my life.

It wasn't in my mind to make myself a gunman, but in my business I had need of one; sometimes in a hurry. I also knew because of my business, that my soul needed nourishment.

CHAPTER 7 – Austin

We arrived in Austin, a city of now over 10,000 inhabitants around mid-morning. Reconstruction, despite its problems, had been good to the city of Austin. New, solid masonary structures had replaced the wooden buildings. Recently, the state established the city as the undisputed capital.

Hidalgo and I rode down Congress Avenue. Goodness, the town was bustling. Horses and wagons up and down the street and something that was called a mule car transported passengers to different locations along the street, plus there was a host of people moving around on foot. This was only the second time I had been in Austin, the first being five years ago when I came with Doak Waters, Hidalgo and Miles Forrest.

It was almost more than I could take in. I remembered Memphis, from years back, and how busy it was.

Looking over at Hidalgo. "What's say we get somethin' to eat and camp outside town? The meetin's not 'til tomorrow."

We rode up a little closer to the capitol and saw a sign--"Beulah's Fine Dining." I wasn't quite sure what a diner was but I could see tables inside.

"Let's try it," I said. We stopped, dismounted, and tied the horses to the hitching rail.

As we walked in we noticed that the few customers were dressed, I'll say, more elegantly than the two of us. I was not sure what was happening, but the folk were staring at us. We headed for a table and were intercepted by a dandy-looking man with a smirk on his face. I didn't cotton to him at all.

"May I help you?" he asked.

"Hidalgo and I were hopin' to get a bite to eat."

His eyes went to Hidalgo with disdain. "His kind eat a few blocks over."

My eyes met his, "What do you mean, 'his kind'?"

I could feel the tips of my ears begin to burn when a voice yelled out. "Elias, Benito, come on over here an' sit down." It was McNelly; sitting with him was John Armstrong, often called "McNelly's Bulldog." He was usually to be found somewhere near the Captain. Miles was also sitting there, all fancied up.

"Bring them some coffee," ordered McNelly. "Sit down."

Coffee was brought to us and a couple of menus. Hidalgo and I looked at each other after a glance at the menu. This was going to dig deep in my pocket; $.75 for a steak. Goodness, this was Texas, there was beef everywhere. I broke down and ordered steak; Hidalgo ordered liver and onions for $.40. He was more frugal than me. McNelly and Armstrong had large steaks. Then I looked at Miles. He caught my eye and smiled. All he was eating was a piece of pie.

During dinner I briefed the Captain on what happened up at San Angelo. He never lost attention except the one time he began to cough. When I told him of Ty he nodded and looked at Armstrong.

After another round of coffee, McNelly stood. With that we took our cue that dinner was over and it was time to leave. I could have drunk another cup, but I thought I should leave with the others. Looking back I saw some money on the table and started back.

Miles saw me and grabbed me arm. "That's called a tip. Seems like something that's expected when you eat here.

Hidalgo and I went to our horses. I noticed Armstrong pull Miles aside as Captain McNelly walked up to us. Looking at us with that expression on his face--the look of scolding he said, "Hidalgo, Butler," I noticed he used our last names this time. "Always be aware of your surroundings. Whether it be trailing an outlaw or entering an establishment of fine food." He stared for a moment then joined the others.

I looked at Hidalgo. "I think we have just been chastised."

We mounted and rode out of town. Austin had already damaged our financial resources so we weren't about to spend the night in town. Plus, both of us preferred to be out-of-doors. Besides the expense, there were just too many people.

CHAPTER 8 – McNelly's Instructions

McNelly arranged for the meeting of his new Rangers to be held at the Presbyterian church. Now, I didn't know what Presbyterians really were; I had heard of them, of course. Back in Tennessee we all attended a community church with usually a Baptist preacher. However, upon arriving at the church I knew they must be something. It was a grand edifice.

I didn't know if Captain McNelly was Presbyterian or not. I did know he was a very religious man. Someone had told me that he planned on becoming a preacher until the War Between the States. Guess that war had a way of changing a person's plans and often changing the person.

John Armstrong was at the door and today he was all business. "Butler, Hidalgo," he nodding as he acknowledged us and opened the door. "Hats off and watch your spurs."

The meeting was scheduled for 10:00 and Hidalgo and I were early, but there were already a couple of dozen men inside. We all knew the Captain's demands for being on time.

Men were standing in the back with only a whisper or two of conversation. I noticed a small, frail man up front kneeling in prayer. A few more men appeared, then precisely at 10:00 Armstrong came in and shut the door behind him. The man praying stood up, coughed a little, and turned toward us. It was McNelly.

"Gentlemen," came Armstrong's voice from behind us. "Take a seat," and again he reminded us to watch our spurs.

There was quite a bit of anxiousness among us as we settled into the pews. I figured there may be thirty men or so present.

McNelly started to speak. "Welcome men. You have been especially chosen to be part of the new Texas Rangers; the State Police is no more." There were some murmurs amongst the men.

"You have been chosen to represent the State as a newly formed law enforcement agency. You will be paid $33 a month in state scrip. You must furnish your own weapons, the State of Texas will provide ammunition."

"I will," McNelly was interrupted as a late-comer entered the room. I was looking at the Captain and saw his jaw clinch.

"Biggs!" The man looked surprised that McNelly knew his name. "You're late; don't even bother to sit down I have no use for a man that can't keep an appointment."

"Now, just a minute, Captain. I had good reason...."

"Sergeant Armstrong, help Mr. Biggs find the door."

Armstrong grabbed him by the arm. Biggs jerked away. "Don't touch me! I'll be leavin' when I'm ready!"

The swiftness of it startled us. The right arm of Armstrong struck out and the crack of a fist on a chin resounded in the quiet room. Down went Biggs.

Armstrong looked over at Miles. "I think he's ready to leave now. Help me get him out."

Within seconds Biggs was thrown out the door. We heard coughing and our attention was drawn back to

McNelly.

It took a minute or so for the Captain to quit coughing. "Let me continue. I will give you until 5:00 this afternoon for you to make up your mind. If you choose to sign on, most of you will accompany me south of the Nueces."

I saw McNelly nod at Armstrong. "Hidalgo, Brown, Butler, you stay. The rest are dismissed."

Rather quickly the room emptied. The three of us sat there in silence wondering what was going to happen. McNelly started to walk over to us when he again started to cough.

"I want to wait for John to join us before I begin, so relax a few minutes."

He looked at us. "Do you two know Tom?"

We knew who he was, but really didn't know him.

"He will be in charge of your mission. When Albright gets better he will join you."

We heard footsteps on the wooden floor accompanied by the jingle of spurs. In a moment John Armstrong loomed over us. "Sit down, John. I'll give a background and John will fill you in on particulars."

"I'm taking the others down into the Rio Grande Valley. There have been rustlers moving back and forth across the border and it seems that most of it is instigated by Juan Cortinas," he paused and I thought he was going to start coughing again.

"You," and he pointed at each of us, "are going to investigate further upriver. About halfway between Laredo and Del Rio is a community that bears our scrutiny. Sergeant...."

"The town is called, 'Mal de Ojo,'" began Armstrong.

Hildalgo sat up straight and whispered, "Evil Eye."

"Yes, Benito, the town is called Evil Eye and you are going to find out why. As with Cortinas' outfit, the town is on the Mexican side of the Rio. When you go there you'll be on your own. Help won't be near, but there will be a contact in Laredo and also at the King Ranch.

"Hidalgo, you'll leave tomorrow. We want you there a month before Brown and Butler show up. You'll be a spy, so to speak. They will join you in a month. There are rumors of an operation there that preys on this side of the border. It is not as well known as Cortinas; that's why we want you to check it out."

"Do we have a name?" asked Brown.

"One name that has been mentioned is Markel Ceron. They seem to be very secretive," stated Armstrong.

"There will only be the four of you, so Brown is now acting corporal. Sorry, Tom, no pay raise."

McNelly began to cough. I looked at Armstrong and could see the concern in his eyes.

"Both of these missions are vital to the State of Texas," said McNelly with iron in his voice. "The first is to protect the innocent from the vicious prey of evil men. The second is to reestablish the Texas Rangers as an honest, law enforcement group for the State."

Armstrong stood up as did the Captain so we took it as our cue to get up and leave. As we stood McNelly spoke. "Do your duty; defeat evil where you see it and go with God. I'll be praying for you."

CHAPTER 9 – McNelly Is Confronted

The three of us huddled together to find a time when we would meet. Hidalgo would leave immediately and I told Brown I would be at his place in twenty days. That would give us just under two weeks to get to Mal de Ojo. Hopefully Hidalgo would have some information for us when we arrived.

As Hidalgo mounted, I went over to him. "Benito, you be careful," I paused and gave a deep sigh, "I don't think this will be easy; go with God."

He gave that wide, toothy smile of his. "You too, my good amigo."

Then our attention was drawn to a commotion in the street. "McNelly!" came the scream. "You shamed me! Come out and face me!"

It was Biggs, half-stumbling down the street with an almost empty whiskey bottle in his left hand, and a cocked pistol in his right.

"McNelly!"

Then I saw the Captain appear. Armstrong attempted to step to the street but the Captain put up his hand to stop him. Stepping out to face Biggs he opened his coat, and then turned with his frail, thin body to the side, giving a smaller target. He was fully composed.

To my right there was a sudden movement. It seemed as if Miles came out of nowhere and with his left hand grabbed the wrist of Bigg's hand that held the pistol. Like lightning with his right hand flush into the face of Biggs he threw three jabs that sounded like an axe hitting cordwood. Holding him up with his left hand Miles gave a mighty kick to the groin, and released him to fall to the ground. Stooping down he picked up the pistol from where Biggs dropped it, then reached for the bottle of demon-juice and poured it into the street.

"Forrest, you didn't have to interfere," said McNelly.

"Just figured I'd save you some grief, Captain. No need for a fella to get kilt over stupidity."

"Plenty of grief came my way during the War," McNelly replied.

There was a moment of silence as their eyes met. "Understood, but there's no need to add to it today. Figured you'll earn some down in the Valley."

McNelly nodded and Miles turned to me. "Elias, take care."

"You do the same."

Brown and I mounted; McNelly, Armstrong and Miles walked on down the street. After we parted and starting on our separate ways, I took a glance back; Biggs was still lying in the street.

I gave Fred a little kick to urge him to move a little faster and headed northeast out of Austin. My idea was to ride to Cameron figuring I should make it in five days or so. It had been a while since I had ridden alone as I had become so used to riding with Hidalgo; I was going to miss his cooking.

The saddle I was mounted on had sure seen better days. My plan was to go to old Carl Schluntz's and see Alejandro about making me a new one. I didn't want anything fancy, but I had seen some of his work a few years back and had a yearning for one of his saddles.

Fred and I headed on out of town on the road toward Waco. I didn't know that Captain McNelly was soon to face one of the largest struggles of his life; and, for that matter, so was the reconstructed State of Texas. I thought a bit about what might be in front of me, but soon put that thought aside. A man gets to thinking and feared about tomorrow and most of the time that's all it amounted to— fear.

CHAPTER 10 – Visitor in Camp

Normally, I don't do much singing while riding, especially the back country, but I was out on a well-traveled road and feeling good so I cut loose, "This is my story...." I noticed Fred shake his head a few times as if there were flies buzzing around. Finally, he turned his head around and chomped at my leg.

"Wha...!" I exclaimed. He shook his head again. "Is it you don't care for my singin'?" Then I heard a snort.

"Well, I think I sound pretty good." He shook his head again. "Ha, lot you know 'bout good music. For the sake of you delicate ears I'll just hum a mite."

It was the third night on the trail. I had about a day, day and a half before reaching Cameron. I camped off the road a couple hundred years, a little earlier than usual. Finishing a supper of bacon and dried apples I settled back to drink coffee and pulled out my Bible. I turned to the Gospel of Mark and began to read.

"For from within, out of the heart of men, proceed evil thoughts, adulteries, fornications, murders, thefts, covetousness, wickedness, deceit, lasciviousness, an evil eye...."

That struck me. Funny, I know I've read that passage before, but never noticed that one of the sins mentioned was "an evil eye." That's where McNelly was sending us, Mal de Ojo, "Evil Eye."

After drinking another cup of coffee I settled down on top of my bedroll for the night. I might have just dozed off but felt a presence in the camp; my hand went to the butt of my gun.

Sitting up I looked around. "Elias." Hearing my name I pulled my gun. "Elias, put the gun away." There was a voice, but I didn't see anyone. My heart was a-pumping but I felt strangely at peace as well, so I holstered my pistol.

Glancing at the fire I noticed flames, but when I went to bed it was only glowing with hot coals. Also strange, there was no additional wood.

"Elias," the voice seem to come from the flames. "Extreme difficulties lie before you. Be strong and courageous. I AM with you!" With those final words the flame disappeared and all I saw were the hot coals.

Now, I'm not one to hear voices nor to believe in a bunch of mumbo-jumbo, but something mystical had happened here. I moved back to my bedroll and laid down. My mind went to Moses and a bush that burned. I didn't think I'd sleep, but the next thing I knew the dawn was breaking. Seldom does the sun beat me up, but it had today.

Leaning over the firepit I started stirring the ashes to find some hot coals. I added a little tinder and then fanned them with my hat. Within a few seconds there was a flame. I added some small sticks so I could get a fire started for coffee.

After eating a few slices of bacon and drinking a few cups of coffee I completed my morning ritual. Saddling Fred, I took him to the stream; he had foraged during the night. I mounted and started to ride off, but turned to

look at the place where I camped. I shook my head—
something had happened here last night or I was going
daft. Touching Fred lightly with my spurs he took off at a
brisk trot.

I was closer to Cameron that I thought; by late
afternoon I rode into town. It suddenly hit me, Schluntz
may not even have a shop anymore. It had been several
years since I was last here. The town hadn't grown much
and I thought I remembered where his shop was. I rode
down main street a couple of blocks, then took a side
street to the north, then followed the next street as it
turned back parallel to Main. There it was: Gun & Saddle.

I dismounted and looped the reins over the post. A
little bell gave notice to my entering. I saw Schluntz bent
over, working on a firearm at his bench.

"Be with you in a minute."

I browsed at the guns on the wall and in the display
case. He turned and took a few steps toward me.
Stopping, he squinted, then pulled his glasses from his
forehead over his eyes.

"My young friend who carries the small cannon.
Welcome! Welcome!" He clasped his hands and then
clasped my shoulders and looked in my face. "Ah, but not
so young anymore. Experience is etched on your forehead
and in your eyes; your eyes resemble those of Stiles."

He paused, "Speaking of my friend Stiles, how is he?"

"Dead."

"No, I cannot believe it. Do you know how it
happened?"

"He was shot down in the streets of Abilene."

"That cannot be. Not Stiles. No one could take him
with a gun."

"I was there, I saw it. He was surprised and he wasn't
wearing a gun." There was a puzzled look on Schluntz's

face. "Abilene has this law, no guns to be worn in town. Stiles was unarmed and goin' to get his gun when it happened."

The old gunsmith sat down, seemingly aged even more by the news. "Hard to believe," he said. "He was a good friend. But we all have our time."

He turned to me, wiping his hand across his face and asked, "Are you still carrying the Remington?" I nodded and pulled it from my holster. "May I see it, please?"

I handed it over to Carl and nodded toward the back. "I really would like to see Alejandro about a saddle. I'm practically ridin' bareback with the piece of leather I've got."

He smiled as he fondled my gun, "Go on back, Elias. I want to check out your pistol."

I moved on through the doorway and the sweet smell of leather filled the air. Alejandro was by the back door working in the light that it offered. It was a double door so it would give him more light.

He called out, "Senor Butler, good to see you again. How may I be of help?"

"Lookin' for a saddle; mine is thinner than worn out shoe leather. In fact there is a hole startin' to wear through and the cantle is completely broken down."

I saw him give a big toothy grin similar to Benito's. "I have three for sale and I think one of them will suit you just fine. If you do not like, I'll make a custon one jest for you. Come, look."

There were three saddles on display. One had the big Mexican horn which I immediately discarded in my mind. The one next to it was a beautiful saddle. Alejandro must have spent much time engraving on it, but too fancy for Fred; it would make him uppity. He was standing in front of the last one, blocking it from view and smiling.

After a few moments he moved away. "This is the one for you, Senor!"

It was light brown, but then I noticed something on the back of the pommel, there were two stones, one whitish with red streaks, the other a reddish color with darker red speckles. They had been enlaid on the saddle. I couldn't take my eyes off them.

"You like?" he asked smiling. "These stone were very special to my grandmother. She kept them to ward off the 'evil eye.'"

I looked at him startled. "What did you say?"

"These stones are called 'bloodstones', and it is said they can block the evil eye from gaining a hold on your soul."

"Mal de Ojo," I said in whispered tone.

"Si, *mal de ojo*, you have heard of it? People from my old country are very superstitious; they believe in the evil eye seeking their soul."

"How much?"

He grinned that big grin again, "For you, my friend, $70, but not in script."

"That's twice as much as my horse!"

"I saw your horse," he said with a laugh. "This saddle is definitely worth twice as much as, what you call a horse."

I walked back in the other room and Schluntz was finishing wiping down my gun.

Alejandro followed me. "You no want saddle?"

"I want it, just can't afford it."

Carl handed me my pistol. "I cleaned it good and made a slight adjustment to the pull of the trigger. You might want to try it a few times to get the feel before having to put it to the test."

"How much?" I asked and he waved his hand at me.

"Just protecting my workmanship."

"Hold on a minute." I walked outside and to my saddlebag. I grabbed a parcel and walked back in to Alejandro. "How about $30 and you hold on to this ol' Walker Colt? I'll come back within a year and pay off the rest."

I saw out of the corner of my eye Carl nodding. "Deal, Senor Elias. I'll get your saddle."

In a few minutes he had taken it outside and was taking off my ragged old one.

Carl grasp my shoulders and looked me in the eyes. "Elias, go with God."

Just before mounting I put my fingers across one of the bloodstones. I waved goodbye and gave Fred the nudge of a spur.

CHAPTER 11 – Tom Brown

It had been six days on the road when I rode into Tom Brown's place. He had a nice little spread; barn was solid as was the corral. It was well kept up, and the impression struck me that this was a man who knew what he was doing.

As I approached the front of his little house, there was some noise from the back that sounded like hammering.

"Anybody home?" I yelled.

A few seconds later a woman opened the front door and peered out. "Howdy-do, ma'am. Name's Elias Butler and I'm lookin' for Tom Brown."

She opened the door wide and I saw a tall, rather large, but good-looking, brown-haired woman. Her hair was pulled back; she was wearing a gray dress with an apron over it and holding a pistol. Seems to me that most women here in Texas answer the door wearing an apron and holding a gun.

"Mister Butler, get down. We've been expecting you. Tom's around the back working on the house. I'll go 'round with you."

Dismounting, I threw the reins over the only hitching

rail and walked back with the lady I assumed was Mrs. Brown. Turning the corner there was Tom hammering away at what looked like the wall of an additional room.

"Tom! Stop that racket! We have a guest."

"Well, it's 'bout time you show'd up Butler. I was headin' out in a few days whether you were here or not."

Now I didn't know the fellow very well, but to my way of thinking, he wasn't all that friendly, much less polite.

"Sarah, take him to the porch. I'll be 'round in a few minutes; I'm almost finished here."

"Come on, Mr. Butler. I'll get you a cup of cool water."

"Elias, ma'am. Let me take care of Fred and I'll be there."

"Fred?"

"My horse, ma'am."

"Funny name for a horse."

"I think so too, but he kinda likes it."

She smiled and I could see why Tom was smitten by her. "Take him to the trough by the windmill, and Elias, it's Sarah."

"Yes, ma'am, Sarah."

After giving Fred his drink and unsaddling him I walked up to the porch where Sarah was waiting with a cup of water. She handed me a nice ceramic cup with some kind of blue design on it, then sat down in a rocker.

I tried to get my finger through the handle, but couldn't make it fit so just held the cup in my hand. "Ahhh, that's refreshin', especially it bein' so hot today."

"We have a good well, and the water is right cool. Tom dug it right off the kitchen so I wouldn't have to go far."

Tom had a house that was well-built, a solid barn and corral, and a beautiful, if somewhat plump wife; yep, he

42

had done quite well. Many Texans hadn't fared so well after the War. Reconstruction had taken a toll on Texas with many a Carpetbagger and Scalawag lining his pockets. Widows were especially hard hit; husbands killed during the war, they couldn't hold onto their farms and ranches.

'Shore a nice place here, ma'...Sarah. How long you and Tom been married?"

"Going on six years now," came her reply.

"Hmmmm."

"Did you say something Elias?"

"I was just a-thinkin' 'bout your ranch." What I was really thinking was she was fortunate he had survived the War. I just missed it, and I'm sure he was a few years older than me.

The War wasn't brought up in casual conversation. Southerners still felt the pain and shame, but it made me wonder. Then I heard Brown's footsteps coming around the side of the house and stepping on the wooden porch. It brought me out of my pondering.

"All framed in," he said moving over to Sarah and giving her a hug. "I'll finish it up on the inside as soon as we get back." He looked over at me. "You are all rested up, aren't you, Butler?"

Now, I don't know why he was trying to irk me, but it was starting to come on, so to break away I said. "I'm goin' to go brush down Fred."

Sarah stood up and was walking back inside, and turned to say, "I'll go finish supper. It won't be long."

"Turn your horse loose in the corral. You can pay me two-bits for feed," he paused looking me in the eyes. "I'll take script."

My eyes narrowed with my reply, "Hospitable."

He didn't respond so I walked away and picked up the reins, "Come on, Fred."

I spent a little more time than normal feeding and brushing him down. Long enough to settle my thoughts, and cool down my simmerin' gizzard. I went ahead and threw my bedroll in the barn. Wonder if he'll charge me for lodging.

I was muttering to myself when I heard Sarah call, "Supper."

Coming inside I wasn't surprised. It was built as solid as the outside. As I entered I was directed to my right to a room with a table and chairs. The table was all spread with some fine dishes. The same sort as the cup I drank out of.

"Let me take your hat, Elias, and have a seat."

Now, I don't know if she was showing off for company or not, but we had pork chops, pintos, some kind of greens she called spinach, and fried onions, along with a large hunk of cornbread. There was plenty of coffee, and my eyes lit up for she finished off supper by bringing in a custard pie.

There wasn't much conversaton during supper. I started to bow my head to say grace, when Sarah gave a little cough and I saw Tom sneer at me. Then we ate, and Tom wolfed down his food as if he had been starving.

"What yuh buildin', Tom?" I asked trying to start some conversation.

He finished his last bite of pie, wiped his mouth with his sleeve. Sarah got up to get his plate, and he took hold of her hand and pulled her to him. "New room for my son," and he reached around and patted her stomach.

Dummy me, she wasn't plump, she was with child. I looked at her and she was blushing. "Let me go, Tom."

"That's why we're leavin' before first light. I want to be gettin' back."

"No breakfast?" I asked softly in sort of a whiny voice.

Mal de Ojo

CHAPTER 12 – On the Trail with Tom

I reckoned it was around 4:00 a.m. or so by the time I had Fred grained and saddled and headed up to the porch. I wanted to be waiting when Brown came out as I had heard some movement in the house.

It must have been close to an hour later, and I figured graylight was not far off when I finally heard some more movement and the sound of voices. The minutes went by; finally the door opened and Brown came out drinking a cup of coffee. Shutting the door behind him, he took one last swallow, set the cup down and headed to the corral for his horse.

Not a "good morning," not even a nod; that was about as low-down as I've seen a man get. Why, I've arrested outlaws who would at least share their coffee with me.

Brown was mounted and heading my way. As I started to mount the door opened.

"Elias, I made some biscuits, and there's a chop from last night."

Sarah stood there with a small poke in one hand and holding her wrapper together with the other.

"Obliged, Sarah," I said tipping my hat then reaching out for the package.

I was mounting Fred when she softly said, "Bring him

back safe to me, Elias."

"That'll be my plan," I said in return.

"Are you going to ride or stand there gawking at my wife in her night clothes?" asked Brown with disgust in his voice.

He was headed on down the road when I finally got mounted. "Sarah," I said again and waved. "Come on, Fred, yahaw."

I caught up with him right quickly and was munching on one of those biscuits. My innards were a-hankering for a cup of coffee, but the biscuit was going to have to do.

"She got up early to make those biscuits for you."

"Figured as much. They're right tasty. Didn't you get one?" and I offered him the other one.

"I had my breakfast," he said and put a spur to his horse.

My goodness, what is wrong with this guy? He seemed fine back in Austin a month ago, but since I had been at his place I found him sort of surly.

It was a long six-day ride to Del Rio. He was sullen around camp at night. He sure didn't have a mind to help out with camp chores. I made the coffee and was sure to fill my cup first.

He didn't say much the whole trip. Complained mostly, when he did speak of how hot it was, how McNelly had been unfair to him, about only being a corporal. He complained on how I cooked the bacon, or about that chili powder I put in the beans, or that my coffee was too strong.

I was always up before him going off to practice my draw and do my reading. I was walking back into camp one morning when he asked, "What's that book you're reading?"

"My Bible," I replied. "Always try to get some of it in

my system even if I do miss breakfast now and then."

"It's bad enough that McNelly is a Bible-toter, now he's saddled me with another one."

"Maybe he figured you needed the help," I said trying to be light.

"Bah!"

Later on that day, trying to be congenial and work on some kind of relationship, I mentioned to him. "You sure have a nice place, Tom."

"My father and I worked hard enough to get it," he replied gruffly.

I hadn't heard anything of his father so I continued the conversation. "Father in the War?"

"Not really your business, but yes, in the navy." Before I could ask he added, "I worked with him." And that was the end of the conversation.

The last day on the road I suggested we camp early and ride into Del Rio the next morning.

"Not me! I want a saloon and a look at those pretty senoritas!"

"Tom! What are you sayin'? You're married, and soon to be father."

"Sarah's six days away."

"You're beginnin' to digust me, Tom," I said and spat for emphasis. "I'll be camped south of town on the Rio Grande. I'll be headin' out in two days."

"Don't you be worrying, holy boy. I'll be there to do my job." He gave his horse a nudge with the spur and galloped on.

I stopped and dismounted, as I had a bitter taste in my mouth. Hoisting my canteen I took a long drink, then checked my supplies. Figured I would be there shortly after noon so would stop, resupply, and travel south along the river.

Del Rio was an active little farming community. They must be very industrious for there were several canals dug for irrigation. Looking up the street I saw a sign, "Mercantile—John Perry." Riding up to it I dismounted and threw the reins over the hitching rail. Fred didn't need to be tied.

Perry had a nice store for a village of this size with a large window to let in light. The smells of wheat and other grains were inviting. I mosied through the store, just looking and then went over to the counter to make my order: coffee, bacon, and some beans; then I saw some of those peppers that Hidalgo would grind and picked up a dozen of those. The bill came to $1 exactly.

"What's this?" he asked.

"That's genuine State of Texas script payable for all purchases made by Texas Rangers." I could see the doubt rise for his forehead began to wrinkle, so I showed him my little badge. "You could also bill the office up in Austin."

He decided to accept it, and tried to get me to eat next door. "Best chili in town, but they won't take your script."

I was sorely tempted, for I have a weak spot for good chili, but I didn't want to run into Brown while in town. Perry informed me that there was a little town a couple days ride south, name of Eagle Pass.

While we were in conversation I asked, "Mal de Ojo, every heard of it?"

Perry's eyes widened. "You don't want to go there. From what I hear, it's a very wicked place."

"Hear anything else?"

"Heard they run stolen goods across the river a few miles north of here and then take them down the Mexican side."

"Why so far, if it is south of Eagle Pass?" I asked a

49

little confused.

"Not even El Diablo wants to tangle with King Fisher. At least not yet."

CHAPTER 13 – King Fisher

Brown didn't show. I was two nights on the trail in good company—myself. At least I didn't have to put up with his foul attitude.

I didn't hurry along for I needed some time to ponder. El Diablo, that name was metioned by the outlaw I killed back in San Angelo. Hmm, stolen goods, not just cattle taken from Texas.

King Fisher, sure I had heard of him. Most people in Texas had, especially law officers. He knew how to walk the line, and there was talk that he would raid into Mexico, or so I overhead McNelly say. He was said to be good with a gun, some said a killer. I was good with a gun, and I had killed men—did that make me a killer? Guess there is a line to be drawn there as well.

Since I had a slow start, it was late afternoon when I arrived at Eagle Pass and still no Brown. The town was very small: store, hotel, a few saloons. I figured I'd spend the night in the hotel and give Fred a good feed in the stable. Hopefully, Brown would show up. I wasn't going to stay more than two nights.

I checked my supplies, and before going back to the hotel I stopped at the store for more ammunition. I should have purchased a few boxes at Perry's, and I certainly didn't want to be caught short. The Captain said the Rangers would supply the ammunition, but I was the only Ranger in the vicinity.

The store owner was cordial, but he wouldn't accept Ranger script. I had to dig into my own pockets for the few dollars that were hidden there. Then I went up to my room in the hotel to drop my purchase off. It was nigh unto evening and my stomach was starting to make peculiar noises. There was a cantina next door so I went in to get a bite.

There was a small section with four tables that opened into a larger room which was the saloon. The saloon was fairly well lit, but the section with the tables was quite a bit darker. Each table had one small candle. Being dark like that made me wonder about the food. Maybe they didn't want you to see what they were feeding you.

My stomach said to "never mind" so I sat down and looked at my money. I had two-bits so I ordered some pintos. When my plate came it was loaded with beans and some other type of concoction covered with what sort of looked like chili with plenty of them jalapenos.

"Hey, I didn't...," and was stopped before I could finish.

"Compliments of the house," came a voice. A man, about my size, walked up to the table. "Mind if I sit?"

He was taking the chair as I nodded my agreement. I noticed a man with him who stood a few feet away and to his back.

"Go ahead, eat. I like to watch a man eat his last meal."

The fork stopped about halfway to my mouth and I lifted my eyes to look at him.

"No, no, the food's fine," he laughed. "I mean you're not staying long in Eagle Pass, so enjoy. By the way, they're called enchiladas."

I will say they were quite tasty. After swallowing several mouthfuls I asked, "D'ya have any coffee?"

"What, no beer?" asked the man.

"Don't drink the stuff," I said looking at him.

"Interesting," he muttered. "So why, my new friend, all the ammunition?"

That went to tell me that the proprietor must report to him. He was dressed very colorful attire. As I studied him; it was almost like looking in a mirror; we were the same height, and I guessed the same weight. His hair was maybe a little darker. I noticed two differences: he kept his moustache neat and trimmed, while mine sort of drooped into a handlebar shape, and there was a look in his eyes. It was something I had seen once before in the eyes of Stiles; this was not a man to trifle with.

"A man never knows when he might have to shoot up something."

"Ahh, but enough for a small war. Are you planning on shooting up me?" he asked with a smile.

"Mister, I don't even know you," I paused. "And I haven't made up my mind about this being my last meal. " I took a swallow of coffee. "Do you need shootin' up?"

"Some folk might think so. A certain McNelly said he would put me in cuffs."

He saw my eyes widen. "So you know Captain McNelly." This was not a question. "He's a respectable man, but we have some differences of opinion. I'm King Fisher."

"Heard of you, for sure. No, not here for you or to even check you out. I'm waitin' for a fellow Ranger, and if he's not here by day after tomorrw I'm leavin'."

The owner came by to fill up my cup and brought Fisher a drink of some clear-looking whiskey.

Fisher smiled, "I only drink on special occasion, but I reckon every day I'm alive is a special occasion." He lifed his glass toward me.

I touched his glass with my cup. Here was a man I could probably like, given the right circumstances.

"What can you tell me about Mal de Ojo?"

His eyes seem to darken, "Stay away from that place. El Diablo controls it."

"I just want to check out some doin's by a man named Markel Ceron."

"Ceron—El Diablo," said Fisher.

"The devil? He thinks he's the devil?"

"If not the devil, certainly a devil. He is foul and would not stop to do anything despicable or dastardly." He threw his shot glass against the wall and for a moment I saw the anger flare up in King Fisher.

"If you ... by the way, who has McNelly sent out here to his death?"

"Butler, name's Elias Butler."

"Well, Elias Butler, it was prophetic that I call that your last meal. I was sayin' that if you and I would tangle it would be face-to-face. I would shoot you, and then have a respectable burial for you. Not so with Ceron. He would kill you by any means, then slice you up and feed you to the hogs. It would be best if you went back to Austin.

I nodded my appreciation. "I'm just ridin' by his place. How come he hasn't bothered your ranch?"

"Right now I have some good, but hard men ridin' for me. It'll happen, eventually. He steals from the Texans, but crosses the river above Del Rio," he hesitated and looked at me. "Sometimes I cross the Rio and bring the cattle back to Texas."

I started to get up when he stared at me. "My friend, Elias, he doesn't only steal cattle and horses. As I've said he is despicable.

I looked at him and stood up reaching out my hand. "Thanks for the meal...it won't be my last supper," I paused. "And I want to be able to say I shook the hand of King Fisher."

I was still eyeing him, and was ready to withdraw my hand when he smiled and reached out and shook it.

"Elias Butler," he said. "It has been said that Ceron deals in human goods, and also has mystical powers."

"What do you think?" I asked.

"I would say yes, to the slavery, but mystical powers, ha! But he is still very evil and dangerous."

As he released my hand he spoke one more time. "I hope we never have to face each other on opposite sides. Before you leave, stop by the mercantile."

CHAPTER 14 – The Return of Brown

"My last meal," I thought as I walked upstairs to my room. Well, he was wrong there, unless the Lord took me that night, for I fully intended to eat breakfast.

Sitting down on the edge of the bed I tugged at my boots. I looked them over and decided I needed to find a cobbler after I got back to Austin. Problem is I can't leave them with someone or I'd have to walk around barefoot.

"Whew!" I exclaimed to myself as I opened the windown. "Sure is hot in here." I decided if Brown didn't show tomorrow I'd camp somewhere out of town.

I lay on the bed and the next thing I knew it was morning. Not much to do today except wait for Brown to show. After breakfast I'd go over to the mercantile and see what King had left for me.

The morning belied the temperature that it would be later in the day. Surely did understand why Mexicans worked in the morning and took siesta when the sun was beating down. Some thought they were just lazy, but being in the coolness of the shade seemed some kind of smart to me.

As I walked through the doorway of the mercantile I saw the proprietor wave. He must have been watching for me.

He motioned me over and took me by the arm. "Come with me," he looked around nervously, but there wasn't anyone else in the store.

Pulling me to the backroom, he reached down under some blankets and pulled out a bundle wrapped in oil cloth. I opened it and there was several sticks of dynamite. I looked at him with a surpised expression, and he just shrugged his shoulders.

"Tell him I'm obliged."

"He said to tell you that it would be a good idea that no one knows about it, especially El Diablo."

I nodded, "Seems smart."

"Here," and he handed me a small burlap poke. "Let's get a couple more items to put in there with those sticks; folks won't get as suspicious."

"Always can use more coffee," I said with a little chuckle.

"What's so funny?"

"Just thinkin', what if one of those sticks broke and that black powder got mixed with the coffee."

Afterward I went on back to the room to get my gear and check out. As I stepped outside, there came Brown riding down the street.

I stood there as he rode my way. "Butler, where're you goin'?"

"T' get my horse," I paused. "Wonderin' if you'd show up."

I saw a flicker in his eye and his jaw tighten. "I need a drink. Come on, I'll buy you one."

As he dismounted I noticed a good size bruise on his cheek, and his lip was split. "I'm gonna set up camp just south of town. I'll be headin' for Mal de Ojo in the mornin'. " Then I headed for the stable.

A couple of hours later he found the camp. He didn't talk and tried to keep his face turned away from me. I was sitting, propped against my saddle honing a finishing edge to my knife.

"Any coffee?" he finally asked.

"On the fire."

"Where's the cups?"

I raised mine, and took a swallow. He glared at me for a minute then began to rummage through his gear to find a cup.

"We're 'bout a half days ride, maybe a little more," I said.

"How do you know?"

"Man told me," I said touching the blade, then sheathing it. Looking at him, "Looks like you had a rough time. Better get some rest; I've a feelin' it's gonna get rougher."

CHAPTER 15 – A Glimpse into Tom's Life

I was just getting settled and as the night was warm I didn't bother with my bedroll. With the warm night we didn't add any more wood to the fire and now just the coals were glowing.

"You don't think much of me do yuh?"

"Tell you the truth, Brown, it would be better said I don't think of you much at all. You're the one that will have to stand before his Maker. You're the one one that's shaming Sarah.

"There you go with that God stuff again!"

"You asked, I told you," and then there was silence.

I was just getting comfortable when he said, "She wouldn't understand."

"What woman would?" I replied.

"No, the ranch, the life she has; it, it came with a price." There was a moment of silence then he continued. "My father was a captain in the Confederate navy. He ran supplies into Corpus and Matamoros down in Mexico."

"Blockade runner?"

"For a while, but after Vicksburg fell the Yankees didn't pay much attention to the Texas coast. I was in charge of supplies once they were unloaded. We fared well during the war."

"And after?" I asked.

"With the war lost, father knew there would be big changes. We stood the chance to lose everything. I don't think Sarah could've stood losing the house," he sighed.

"Father became involved in politics and got close to those in power."

"Scalawag," I ventured.

"We were called that by some. But father was never crooked. I joined the State Police. That's when I met the Captain."

I think he expected me to say something, but I remained silent.

"There were many that were corrupt in the force, McNelly did his best to keep it running correctly and he made enemies among several. One thing for sure, a man could never doubt his honesty, and loyalty to justice and Texas. I followed him into the Rangers.

"So why Sarah?" I asked.

"The ranch was paid for by Carpetbag money. She doesn't know that. There would be no way to pay for it with wages from the State Police."

"So why Sarah?" I asked again.

It was silent.

Then he spoke softly, "I really don't know. I feel ashamed of doing the things on the edge of the law. I look at her, and then ride off."

"She's better than that," I said. "Sounds to me that you need some Higher help."

I expected a harsh retort, but there was nothing; only the sounds of the night and the hissing of the coals as they began to cool. I closed my eyes.

At graylight I was up and stirred up the coals to find a hot one. Adding a few sticks, a flame rose and I put on the coffee to boil.

Coming back from my normal routine I picked up from Stiles, I was a little surprised to see Brown at the fire cooking up some bacon.

"Whatcha readin' this mornin'?" he asked.

I still had my Bible in my hand and replied. "A little from the Sermon on the Mount."

"Read a portion," he said.

Not to let this opportunity pass by I read. "Blessed are the peacemakers: for they shall be called the children of God."

"Hmmmm, Elias, ain't we peacemakers?" Then there was a sizzle, and Brown exclaimed, "Hot!" as he reached to move the coffe that was now boiling over.

Other than that it was a quiet morning as we drank our coffee and ate. We knew that later that day we would cross into Mal de Ojo.

CHAPTER 16 – A Talk

It was already getting hot when we mounted that
morning. The sky was clear and that meant the intense
heat of the Texas sun would soon be beating down on us.

Not far down the road we came to a fork. There was a
large sign on the road to the left. "King Fisher's Road –
Take the Other Road."

Well, we were taking the other road. Only the good
Lord knew where it would take us.

"Think this Fisher is tough enough to enforce it?"
asked Brown.

I smiled as I replied, "I would say so," then paused for
a few seconds. "Only met one man that is tougher."

"Who's that?"

"McNelly!"

"You think McNelly's tough?" he asked kind of
surprised.

"There's all sorts of toughness. McNelly's got them
all." I glanced one more time at the sign before riding on.

About an hour later we pulled up at a stream with a
trickle of water. We were a short distance from the Rio
and I figured there may be a little pool there. Following
the stream toward the river, we found it so we let our
horses get a good drink.

There were almost no trees around save a few straggly mesquite. There was some catclaw and plenty of brush that I didn't know the names of, also grass and cacti around. Seemed like everything had some kind of thorn on it.

I remembered cleaning deer with thorns imbedded deep in the muscle. How they could run in this country was a mystery to me. Made me admire those brush-poppers who came in the area to find wild cattle.

"Father's probably going to lose everything with the new government in Austin," said Brown out of nowhere. "From what I hear, those that collaborated with Carpet-baggers are going to be taken to task."

"Why don't he pack up now and move out?" I ventured.

"He's a Texican. Worked hard for the state. It would be difficult for him to run."

"A man can always start over," I said thinking of my brother Walker and I leaving Tennessee. "But you said your ranch is paid for?"

"Paid for, they can't touch it unless there is some kind of loophole."

"Sarah know the situation?" I asked.

"She wouldn't understand," he mounted. "We better be ridin'."

"You might just be surprised," I said.

Now, when I was a kid back in Tennessee I knew hot days, but since I've been in Texas I'd come to understand the meaning of "hot." The heat of this day was scorching. I couldn't remember a day hotter than this one.

Tom must have been feeling it as well. "Elias," he said suddenly. "Do you believe in Hell?"

"Sure do," I replied.

"Think it's as hot as this?"

"Most likely, hotter." I looked and up ahead I could see a grove of trees blurred by the heat waves. "Tom, let's pull up under those trees. "We're not in that big of a hurry. The shade'll do us and the horses good."

The branches were high enough that we could get under relatively easily. I unsaddled Fred and gave him a quick rubdown. With this heat I fully understood the afternoon siesta. Grabbing the canteen I laid down with my head on the saddle and took a long, deep drink. The water was warm, but it was wet, and I knew the need of keeping it in my system. I knew an old farmer back in Tennessee who died from sunstroke.

I woke with someone kicking my foot. "Wake up, Elias, time for us to be movin'. You've been sleepin' for two hours."

"What?" I couldn't believe I slept that long. It wasn't like me to fall asleep like that anyway. It galled me with all the trails I'd ridden to fall asleep and have to be woken up.

We saddled our horses and walked them down to the river to drink. Just to the south of us was the road that seemed to run close to the river.

As we mounted Tom spoke. "Elias, want you to know. I really don't bed other women." Then he rode off.

I wanted to say something and caught up with him. "Then, what...."

He waved at me, and shook his head, so I kept quiet.

CHAPTER 17 – Village with No Name

It was early evening when our hot, tired horses moved into this ramshackle village. There was a corral, barn, a cantina, a couple of shacks and a few jacals.

Tom reined up at the cantina while I rode on down to the river's edge. On the other side of the Rio Grande lay Mexico and Mal de Ojo. I couldn't see much from where I was, but it was much more impressive than the tiny village where I found myself. The buildings were of wood, but toward the back I could see a few larger buildings.

I decided to ride a little ways down river; went maybe a couple hundred yards. I spied a large piece of driftwood, and dismounting I reached for the package in my saddlebags. This would be as good a place as any to hide the dynamite.

"Fred, be sure you can find this place again." He kind of shook his head as if to say, "not my problem."

Riding back to the tiny village I took Fred over to the corral and led him to a trough of water.

"Hey!" I yelled. "Anyone here?"

Out of the barn came a boy, bare-footed and dirty. "Senor?"

"How much to feed my horse?"

"Veinto centavos," came his soft reply.

I dug into the pocket of my vest where I kept a little pouch of change. "Will this do?" I asked and flipped him two-bits.

His eyes lit up, and he gave a big smile. *"Si, Senor, muchas gracias."*

Turning, I took off my hat and wiped the sweat from my brow with the sleeve of my shirt and strode over to the dingy cantina. Entering I thought I saw the form of Brown standing at a bar. Most of the light came from cracks in the wooden frame and a few candles placed here and there.

Tom motioned me over; he was drinking the same thing I saw King Fisher drinking in Eagle Pass.

"Let me buy you a tequila, Elias."

I waved him off. "What I would really like is somethin' to eat."

Tom laughed. He looked around and said, "Notice how dark it is? That's to keep you from seeing what you're eating."

"That thought did cross my mind," then I changed the subject. "Do we cross on over this afternoon or wait 'til tomorrow?"

Tom slung the drink into his mouth and swallowed. After wiping his mouth he said. "Might as well go on over. Besides they might have a fandango tonight. Plenty of music, food, and senoritas."

"Let's go. At least I may be seein' what I'm puttin' in my stomach."

The sun hurt my eyes as we went back outside. Tom mounted and I went to get Fred. The boy was there and brought him to me.

Though I already knew, I thought I'd be friendly. "What's the name of the town 'cross the river?"

He took a step backward and gave the sign of the cross. "No, Senor, do not go there. It is a very wicked place; much evil."

"It must have a name," I said.

He crossed himself again and replied. "Mal de Ojo."

"Hmmm, and the name of this village?"

"Thees place—it has no name," he said sort of stuttering.

I saw his eyes go to my saddle and he said in whispered tone. "Maybe the stones will help."

Reaching down with gloved hand I rubbed one of the stones. I smiled at the boy, reached in my pocket for another quarter and flipped it to him. "For your trouble," I said and touched the brim of my hat.

"Pray for us," and turned Fred to go meet up with Tom where he was waiting.

"Senor, I will do so."

As we came to the edge of the river I leaned forward and said to Fred in no uncertain terms. "No shenanigans!" He knew my dread of crossing large rivers.

I gave him a nudge and in we splashed. Thankfully, he was able to walk across and didn't have to swim. As soon as his hooves touched the other bank, it felt as if something slammed into my chest. Fred shook his head and gave a loud snort. He had felt something as well. Looking around there was nothing visible, but I sure enough felt what seemed like a weight thrown against my chest.

CHAPTER 18 – Mal de Ojo

There was a long, steep embankment to climb and Fred seemed hesitant. I had to prod him with a spur and he jumped and churned his way up and then over the crest. There was the village about fifty yards away—Mal de Ojo.

We walked our horses slowly toward the town. There was a mesquite tree here and there, and toward the back center of town a few palms rose up towering over the village. It was almost twice the size of Eagle Pass with a couple of two-story buildings off to the right and back of the palms.

All of a sudden, Fred gave a scream and reared up almost throwing me off. After he came back on all four legs he was snorting and agitated. I looked to see what caused this reaction; slithering off the side of the road was a large rattler. I pulled my gun.

"Easy, Elias," cautioned Brown.

"I don't like snakes!" And I watched as it went around the builidng looking for shade.

Fred had settled down, and my heart was nearly back to normal, so we continued on down what seemed to be the main street. Tom started to rein in at the first building, a cantina, but I shook my head as I remembered that snake was somewhere in the vicinity.

We passed two more cantinas, what looked to be some kind of inn or hotel, and came to the market to the left of the square where there was also a large fountain. It was the typical border market with peppers hanging along with some kind of meat, probably goat, and who knows what else. Flies buzzing all around. On the table were a variety of peppers laying beside prickly pear, yucca root, and some things I didn't recognize. To the right of the fountain was another larger cantina.

I threw my reins over the hitching post, as I rarely tied Fred and we walked on in. It was not quite as dark as the one across the river, but dark enough that I took a step to my left to give my eyes time to adjust. As I stepped I was ceremoniously greeted by a distinctive rattle. There is the corner, coiled, was another snake.

"Eets better than a watch-dog, si?" said the man behind a long bar.

"No!" I replied sharply and stepped quickly to the bar, bringing a laugh from the tender.

There were a couple of men down at the other end and three tough-looking but well-dressed characters with large sombreroes sitting at a table drinking. I noticed they were taking an interest in us. Rightly so, I figured, as we were the only gringos in the place.

"Have any beer?" asked Tom of the bartender.

"Si, we make it ourselves," the bartender replied with a proud smile.

"Cold?"

"Senor," came the drawn out reply. "Surely you jest."

The bartender, a short, pot-bellied Mexican man with a dark moustache and hair hanging down just over the top of his ears turned to me. "And for you, Senor?"

"Coffee, and somethin' to eat. My belly's been

beggin' my mouth for somethin' for quite a spell."

"Si, we have some excellent chili. I will bring you some."

"Ifn you have any of them flat tortillas I'd like a couple."

As I turned I saw the puzzled look on his face. "*Tortillas*," clarified Tom. "He don't speak the lingo."

I sat down at the table keeping the rough-looking men in front of me. Tom sat to my left, so he could watch who came in the door.

Before long, the barkeep, who told us his name was Ignacious, came with my food. "Gracias," I said, then muttered to Tom. "And you said I didn't know the lingo."

Ignacious stood there waiting. Tom motioned for me to take a bite. I dug into the chili, stirred it a couple of times, and brought a spoonful to my mouth.

Ignacious stood there smiling as the full flavor erupted in my mouth. "*Muy caliente, si?*"

It was hot, but I dipped the spoon in for another bite. After swallowing, I looked at him. "It's a mite warm, but mighty tasty." He smiled that proud grin again and went to get Tom another beer.

"Two's yur limit," I said to Tom. "You already had whiskey at the other cantina."

He glared at me, then smiled and nodded.

We sat there for thirty minutes, while I ate the chili. For some reason it seemed that tension was beginning to build as we got up and made our way outside.

The sun was bright. I was standing just outside the door when those hard cases started out and bumped up against me. I figured it was because I was standing in their way in front of the door, so I moved a couple of steps to give a little more room but the last one did the same thing. He then walked down to where Fred was standing.

Looking Fred over, he smiled, as he came back to gather the reins. "Nice horse," he said. "I think I will take him."

"I wouldn't," I remarked.

Putting his hands on his hips, he asked, "And why is that?"

"He doesn't like you."

That brought a laugh from all three. As he reached for the reins, Fred turned his head and nipped at him. Jumping back, the man swore something in Mexican and glared at me.

"I tried to tell you he didn't like you."

"No horse tries to bite me," he said as he put his hand on the butt of his pistol.

"Don't!"

He turned and drew. I took a step to my right as I drew my pistol. The shots sounded as one. The post off my left shoulder splintered as his bullet hit it—good thing I had taken that step.

My shot didn't miss. The man fell to his knees clutching his throat. There was the look of fear on his face; the blood was seeping through his fingers as he tried to stem the flow from his throat. He tried to say something, but I could only hear a gurgling sound as I took a step forward.

I don't know if he bled out, or drowned in his blood. He pointed at me with a bloody finger then fell to the side.

His friends were stunned, but when he fell they pulled their guns. At the same time I felt something poke me in the back.

"Don't move," came the voice of Ignacious.

Glancing back I saw he had a shotgun jammed into my back. One of the other men came and relieved me of my gun.

"It was self-defense," I said.

"Maybe," said the one who took my gun, "But what I saw was a deputy checking out your horse. You killed a deputy, we must take you to the alcalde."

"Deputy?" I looked for Tom, but he had backed away up in the shadows. "But he was stealin' my horse."

"The alcade will decide." And Ignacious put more pressure on my back as the two men grabbed me by the arms and pulled me toward a building to the back of the fountain.

CHAPTER 19 – Visitor in the Night

The room to which they took me was well lit. There was a chandelier with several candles and two coal oil lamps, one on each end of a large desk.

Behind the desk, standing with his back to me was a relatively tall man dressed in black. He was looking in the glass of a large gun cabinet, but as I glanced I could tell he was looking at me.

He turned and the first thing I noticed was his eyes. They were dark and menacing. He was shaven except for a well-trimmed goatee and thin, pencil-type moustache.

"Is this the man making the disturbance?" he asked still staring at me.

"Si, he killed Salas; murdered him," and placed my pistol on the desk.

This person, whom I assumed was the alcade, picked it up. He moved it from one hand to the other then twirled the cynlinder. He cocked it and pointed it at me. "Nice pistola. Where did you get it?"

"Texas," was all that I replied.

His eyes caught mine and he again glared at me as he pulled the trigger. I didn't flinch as the hammer hit on the spent cartridge, neither did my eyes move from his.

"Salas was my deputy, and he was very fast with a

73

gun. It is hard for me to believe you beat him."

"It was self-defense," I said interrupting him. "He was stealin' my horse."

"You dare contradict this good citizen?" and he pointed at one of the men with Salas, one of the men who brought me in.

"Just speakin' the truth," I replied.

"The thing we must do then is hold you for trial."

"When will that be?" I asked a little impatiently.

"Are you so eager to be convicted and hung?" Salas was one of my best deputies." Then he smiled, "But luck is with you; court will be in session tomorrow."

"Take him to his cell!" he said turning his back on me.

"Why not let me stay at that inn?" I asked shrugging away from the two guards. "I'll show up."

He turned back to me. "The word of a Norte Americano? No, you will be held in the jail."

"At least check Salas' gun!" I was getting a little desperate as well as agitated.

He reached out his hand to receive the gun. Opening the cylinder, he found a spent cartridge. Glancing back at me, he set the gun on the desk. "Doesn't mean anything. It could have been fired at any time."

Then glancing behind me, "What about your friend?"

I didn't know Tom was in the room. I reckoned Ignacious gathered him up and brought him along.

"We're not friends," Tom piped up quickly.

The alcade looked at me and smiled. "Two gringos just happened to meet and ride into Mal de Ojo? Do you take me for a fool?"

He glared at me again, focusing on my eyes. "What about it? Are you his friend?"

"He ain't exactly the friendly sort," I replied.

He glanced over at Tom. "Get out!" Then to the two

guards. "Take this other away!" When he turned the two men grabbed me and ushered me to a hallway that led outside.

Crossing a street they took me to the two-story building I had seen and pushed me down a hallway on the first floor. This looked to be a prison rather than just an ordinary jail.

I looked at the men; one gave a smile showing crooked, stained teeth. The other unlocked the cell, and I was pushed inside.

It wasn't much to look at. The cell was about 5 by 8 with a 9 foot ceiling. The only light that came into the cell was a couple of windows that were just slits in the wall maybe 4 inches wide and 6 inches high. Underneath them was a slab of cement 3 feet off the floor that constituted a bed. I reckoned this was going to be a long night.

About twenty minutes later as darkness was beginning to fill the room, I heard a noise at the bottom of the door. Peering down from the cement bunk I saw a little door open where food was passed to the prisoners. I jumped to my feet on the bunk for through that slot came a large, wicked-looking rattlesnake with its forked tongue flicking in and out of its mouth.

My heart was in my throat, pounding, threatening to choke me. It was getting darker by the minute and I knew the snake would soon be seeking warmth—me. I had no weapon.

"Lord, help me now," I prayed.

Looking down I noticed my spurs. Reaching down I took one off. My spurs had rowels, not the large Mexican kind, but larger than just a nub. I went to the window and began to scrap, hoping to hone some kind of edge. Darkness was really crowding me now; I couldn't wait any longer.

Looking below I could barely make out the snake. I had only this one, slim chance.

"Lord!" and I jumped down hoping my boots would connect with the head, pinning it down.

As I hit I heard a crunch, then reached down with my left hand for the tail. It was moving back and forth, but I grabbed it and with my right hand holding the sharpened spur I began to slash it apart.

It would not be a clean cut, but I was in a frenzy, slashing with the spur. I couldn't see, but felt like it had to be almost through though the snake was still thrashing. I pulled, and it came apart.

I threw what was in my left hand to the corner, and kicked the severed piece that had the head to the other corner. I wanted that deadly head away from me for I knew it could bite even though dead.

Jumping back on the bed I tried to will myself to settle down. Then the thought of it all hit me and I retched spilling what was in my stomach all over the floor.

I sat there, looking toward the door. It was now dark and if they put one snake in my cell they could put another. They most likely would be thinking the first one had done its work.

All I could whisper over and over was, "Thank you, Jesus."

CHAPTER 20 – El Diablo

The next morning I was wakened by the keys turning in the lock. Surpised that I actually slept, I shook my head to get the cobwebs cleared, then went to rub my eyes. That's when I noticed I still had the spur in my hand. All of a sudden, the smell of my vomit and the dead snake hit my nostrils.

The door opened, and I noticed the guards step back due to the smell. One of them was brave enough to peer through the open door, and saw me standing there.

For a moment I could see the surprised look, then he motioned to me to come out and said, "Court in one hour. Let's go, if you want to eat."

They took me to a little walkway between the cantina and the alcade's office. Coming out to the front I spied the fountain and broke away from the two guards.

I dosed my head and began scrubbing at the blood and guts on my arm. One of the guards grabbed me, and I pushed him away and began to clean my off my spur. There was some entrails on my shirt and pants so I soaked my bandana and scrubbed.

The guard I pushed had stumbled but started toward me so I turned to face him, dirty bandana in one hand and spur in the other. The other guard put up his hand to halt him, then spoke to me. "Hurry, if you want to eat."

Soaking my bandana again I scrubbed my arms a little harder; there wasn't much else I could do about my clothes, but at least I cleaned off any chunks. As I stepped to the boardwalk I wadded up my bandana, which was now a rag, and threw it under the walk.

Going into the cantina, this time I took a step to my right. I remembered what lay coiled in the corner to my left; I already had my fill of snakes.

Ignacious smiled as if he were glad to see me, but then I came to the conclusion that he seemed to be always smiling.

"Breakfast, Senor?"

I wasn't really hungry and didn't know if I could actually keep anything down. However, I learned years ago to eat when you had the chance.

Nodding to him I said, "And coffee."

Going to the table I was at yesterday, I sat. One of the guards, the one with the yellow teeth that I had pushed down, leaned against the bar. The other stood by the door, pulling at his moustache and staring at me intently.

A few minutes passed and Ignacious brought the coffee with one of them tortillas rolled up and stuffed with something. I thought it prudent on my part to unroll it and check the contents. It was when I brought my hand to the table I realized I was still holding onto my spur.

After I attached the spur to my boot, I opened the tortilla and recognized eggs, peppers, onions, and refried beans. Satisfied I could eat it; whether it would settle in my stomach was another thing.

After I drank my second cup of coffee the guard at the door came and stood at the table. "Hombre, it is time."

The way he said that made me think of King Fisher and his remark about my "last meal."

There was a large room off to the side of the alcade's office which acted as a courtroom. It was ornately adorned with beams of a reddish-colored wood. Something struck me as out of place, and I pointed it out to the guard.

"It used to be a well; dried up now," he paused. "There is one case before yours."

I thought it quite odd that there would have been a well inside a room such as this.

Suddenly there was a strange feeling that filled the room. "You feel it?" asked the guard noting my discomfort. "The judge, El Diablo, is coming."

Sweeping through a door that must have been his chambers, came a man dressed in black with a wide, red sash around his waist. I was sort of bewildered--shocked would be a good term. It was the alcade. I started to stand and say something when the guard touched my arm and gestured with a finger over his lips, "Shhhh."

He went to his chair and after he sat, his eyes immediately searched mine out. I shook my head, and he gave a sinister smile.

We have two cases before me today. Out of courtesy to the American we will conduct proceedings in Spanish and English.

"Vasco de la Garza, stand!" There was a little man dressed in a dirty, once-white shirt and pants. "There are two counts against you. The first, you were caught stealing. Second, you purposely killed one of the village mascots. State your defense!"

"*Por favor*, my child, she was hungry. Her mother is dead so I took food to feed her," he bowed his head as he spoke and his shoulders stooped lower. He continued, "The snake, it was ready to strike my Contessa." The man was shaking and almost crying now.

"Neither of these offenses carry the punishment of death. On the first, you should have come to me, is that not right?"

"Si," said the shaking man.

"As for the second," said the judge with a sneer, "It was against the snake, the snake will be the judge."

El Diablo snapped his fingers and from the side of the room came two men I hadn't noticed before. They were two of the largest men I had ever seen. Once came and grabbed the poor man and put him in front of the well. The other had a long pole with a hook on one end which he thrust down into the well. He began to stir and soon the sound of rattles filled the room. Pulling the pole out, he stepped back so it would clear the edge of the well; clinging to it was another one of those deadly snakes.

"Reach for the snake; let it judge!"

"No, please, no...." He tried to cower away when the man holding him pushed him toward the snake.

The snake struck, its fangs driving into the cheek of the man. Screaming, the man tried to jump back, but was held firmly. There was blood dripping from the side of his face and then he was pushed forward again.

This time he was able to turn and when the snake struck it hit on top of his right shoulder, near the base of his neck. Both times I winced as I could almost feel the pain.

I saw El Diablo wave, and the large man grabbed the snake at the tail and dropped it back in the dry well. The convicted man fell to his knees, sobbing. He was in that position when he died, either from the poison or his heart just plain gave out.

El Diablo asked in a low voice, but I could pick up what he said. "How old is the child?"

"Five, or so," said the guard who had brought him in.

"She is small, but healthy."

El Diablo gave a nod, "Place her with the others."
Then he turned his gaze to me.

CHAPTER 21 – Trial

"American, stand! Give the court your name!" he exclaimed leering at me.

"Elias Butler, but this is crazy! If you're the sheriff and the judge you could have freed me yesterday. Why waste the time?"

Twice, he slammed the gavel. "You are charged with the murder of Deputy Salas. Sentence will be...."

"Now wait, just a cotton-pickin' minute! Even in Mexico I have a right to defend myself."

I could feel the evil exuding from his eyes as he stared at me. "There is evidence against you. There are witnesses," and he threw my saddlebags on the table. "Empty them!" he ordered one of the big guards.

All my stuff: coffee, bacon, tin cup, my Bible which he picked up and threw on the floor, and some other sundries which he dumped on the table along with a half dozen boxes of ammunition.

He got up and went to the table and stacked the boxes. "So many bullets!"

"Well, it's just not smart to wander around in Texas without enough bullets. There's really not that much: three boxes for my rifle and three for my pistol."

"You thinking about starting a war? Maybe a war

against me?" He took his arm and swooped the boxes off the table, spilling the contents as they hit the floor.

"This is not about bullets or you for that matter. This Salas feller was stealin' my horse, I challenged him. He drew and missed, I didn't. You checked his gun yesterday and saw a cartridge had been fired."

"That could have been fired at any time." He looked to the guard standing by the door. "Did you hear Salas fire?"

"I heard only one shot," he replied.

He then turned his attention to the guard sitting beside me. "His horse, where is his horse?"

"I do not know. I took the saddlebags off to bring them in here. When I went back out his horse was gone."

His eyes honed in on mine again as I spoke. "Let's go to the cantina, I can show you where his bullet hit."

"*Bueno*, let's go," he said. As he started to move the two massive guards fell in beside him.

I was doing a bit of praying as we walked along to the cantina. As we stopped in front of the door, Ignacious stepped outside just as if he had been prompted.

"Ignacious," I stood beside him. "You have a beautiful building. Do you have any damage to your wonderful cantina?"

He gave that big smile. "Oh no, Senor. I check it often and keep it in good repair."

Then I pointed to the post where the bullet from Salas' gun had hit.

"It was not there yesterday," Ignacious proclaimed.

"You're right," then turning my attention to El Diablo. "Not until Salas fired at me."

"Enough!" yelled El Diablo in an almost screeching voice. "Back to the courtroom!"

We went back in and he sat down, behind his long

table. His eyes were cast downward and dark. Finally, after a few seconds, he glanced at me.

"Give him his gun." One of the large guards handed me my pistol. I could tell by the weight that it was unloaded so didn't even bother to check it.

"I do not find you so innocent, but you are free to go. Go back to *Tejas* and do not return!"

I put on my holster and dropped the pistol in it as I was standing at the door. "Francisco! Stand!"

Turning to watch, the two large guards went and stood on either side of the one who had declared that only one shot had been fired. He was beginning to tremble.

Now El Diablo's attention was focused on this guard, Francisco. "I do not mind lying. However, I do not like my court to be found in a lie. Nor do I like to be shamed in front of a gringo, especially by one of my deputies."

He nodded and the large guards picked him up and took him outside and positioned him in front of the stocks. They placed his arms backward into the stocks, then dipped a strap of rawhide in the fountain to wet it wrapping it around his head and fastening it to the post so his head could not move.

"Punishment is—for twenty-four hours, your mouth shall feel the sting of Diablo."

The guard's eyes widened in fear. I could see he had his jaws clamped shut. One of the guards had something in his hand and he ran a piece up Francisco's nostril. I could see it was a stem of some kind as he jammed a second piece up the other nostril. Not being able to breathe he opened his mouth.

The guard now grabbed his jaws and pried, keeping them open while the other thrust a piece of cholla in his mouth. Then he took pieces of wet rawhide and tied his mouth shut.

Francisco's eyes were bulging, and he couldn't breathe. After he was secured, bloody stems were pulled out of his nose.

El Diablo stood in front of Francisco leering into his eyes for a few moments, then turned and went back inside with the large guards following.

I was shaking my head in disgust at the evil thing I had just witnessed. He might live if he could keep from swallowing any of the cholla, but if any of it went into his throat he would suffocate. The guard who had been with me stared briefly at what torture had been given to his cohort, then turned, looked at me, and shook his head.

I walked away, rubbing my moustache and then feeling my throat. My gaze went toward the cantina and there was Fred at the hitching post. Tom was standing just inside the door and when I approached took a step toward the horses.

He handed me the reins to Fred. "I think it's time we ride out of here."

CHAPTER 22 – Fight at the Wagons

Mounting our horses we galloped for the river. I didn't take time to warn Fred of the water and not to pull any shenanigans, so he hit it full speed sending the water splashing up over me. I didn't mind, I just wanted to be across.

When we entered the tiny village with no name, I was fairly well soaked. I knew, however, with that hot Texas sun, I'd dry out quickly.

"Hey, chico!" I yelled, hoping the boy would show up. I wasn't to be disappointed as he walked out of the small shed posing as a barn.

"Water and feed my horse for me?"

"Si, Senor, two-bits," he said with a smile.

That made me laugh. "You learn quick."

We walked to the cantina, but didn't go in. I sat down on a log fashioned as a crude bench, Tom just leaned against the wall. I must have been a mess, soaked, with dried snake guts and vomit on me. I didn't blame him for being upwind.

"I'm worried about Benito," I said after I situated myself on the log.

As I said it Tom straightened. "Don't be, " and he pointed. From downriver, on the Texas side rode Hidalgo.

He looked weary as he approached.

Reining up in front of us he dismounted. I waved to the kid and told him to take care of Benito's horse as Tom stepped inside the cantina and grabbed a couple of chairs.

Benito sat down, looked at me and frowned, then began. "We have to act! Ceron is developing a trade network in Mexico," he stopped and looked at us. "One thing he trades in is slaves he has taken mostly from Texas, women and children."

I thought I had heard screams and crying from the cell, but for all I knew they could have been mine as everything that night was a nightmare.

"Eight wagons left a little while ago with about a hundred women and children."

"We can't do anything about it," said Tom. "We're Texas Rangers and have no jurisdiction in Mexico."

"We're also men!" I declared standing up.

"We have another problem," continued Tom. "Biggs was in the village. He'll sure go to Ceron."

"Biggs is a problem we'll worry about later. Right now we have to help those women and kids."

Benito spoke up. "On the river, south of here, there is a crossing. We can cross there and easily catch up with the wagons before nightfall."

"How many guards?" asked Tom.

"There will be five; there was supposed to be six, but one couldn't make it for some reason."

I had been curling my moustache, "Five guards and eight men on the wagons," hesitating I looked at Benito. "Will the teamsters be armed?"

"I do not think so. They are mostly just peasant workers, but they are deathly afraid of Ceron. To them, he is certainly El Diablo."

"They ought to be. The man is insane. I'm convinced

he believes he is the devil—El Diablo." With that I proceeded to tell Benito and Tom of my ordeal and what happened to the guard who testified against me.

Benito reached out and put his hand on my arm. I don't know why, but for some reason whenever he does that it brings a sort of comfort. "Then surely, he has the devil inside him," he said solemnly.

I looked at Benito. "You look beat. Go lay down for a little while. We can catch those wagons easily; plus the best time would be right as they begin to camp." Then I stood. "That will give me time to go dig up some bullets."

I went to my little cache and within the hour we were on our way. Riding down the dim trail on the American side of the Rio we traveled for about three miles before we crossed. We didn't talk much; each man rode with his own personal thoughts going through his mind.

In a spell, I rode up beside Benito. "What do you know about the 'evil eye'?"

"Not much. I know my *abuelos*, my mother's parents were very superstitious and kept the stone, but my father and his father, oh no...they would fight the devil himself."

"Well, my friend, you may get to do it for them."

"Ceron boasts that soon he will be bigger and stronger than Cortinas and will take him over." Benito looked at me and stopped riding. "He even believes that Texas, south of the Nueces will soon belong to him."

Nudging our horses we quickly caught up with Tom. After crossing the Rio we followed Benito. If possible the land became drier and the sun hotter. We rode for several hours before coming to a road.

We stopped and looked closely at the road. It had not been traveled recently. "This is the road they will travel," said Benito. "We will ride back toward the village on it, but we must be on the lookout for the wagons. I would think they maybe, say, an hour away."

We rode easy and carefully. There was some brush, but mosly the land was filled with large areas of cacti. With very few rises in the land, if we were not careful we might be spotted. I was a little concerned that they might send a rider out further as a scout. Dusk was approaching when Benito stopped.

"Just ahead, there is a little arroyo. There may be some water in it, but doubtful. It would be a good place to camp. Let me circle around and come from the village side."

Benito left us and we continued on a little further before dismounting. Grabbing our rifles, we went ahead on foot. Approaching the edge of the arroyo we could see the glow of fire. Peering over the edge we saw two fires; it looked as if the guards were at one of the fires and the teamsters at the other. Those they were transporting were still in the wagons.

A guard who must have been in charge, was motioning to the others. They got up and went to the first two wagons. Opening the back they were yelling for the occupants to get out. A dozen or so kids of various ages exited cautiously. They were taken 'round to the water barrel and each given one drink from a cup then thrown back in the wagon.

The first two were loaded with children and the last six with women. After they went through the same ritual with each wagon, the guards kept one woman out of the last wagon and bringing her back to their fire. She was young, blonde, and terrified.

They didn't notice a horseman approach. "El Diablo wouldn't like that." It was Benito; he had ridden into camp and caught all of them unawares.

"A little fun is all," replied the guard who grabbed the

woman. "Besides, he will never know."

"El Diablo will know," said Benito, with assurance. "In fact, he is probably watching you right now and will be waiting for you when you get back."

With that the guard let go of the woman and she quickly ran back to her wagon. "These guards were not the brightest," I thought to myself.

Then the one who seemed to be in charge finally figured out there was a mounted man in camp that was not part of their outfit. "What are you doing here?" he demanded of Benito pulling his gun.

"El Diablo sent me. He said you were short one guard."

That didn't quite convince the head guard. "Why should I believe you? Why are we short a guard?"

Benito was good. He gave a great sigh and said, "Seems like one came down with mouth problems; like I might add you seem to be doing. Plus I knew where to find you."

I glanced at Tom; he was taking aim. "No," I whispered forcefully. "That would be murder."

He glared at me, but lowered his rifle. As he did he banged the barrel against the rocky ledge. The guards turned as one to look in our direction.

At least that glance gave Benito the chance to pull his gun. The head guard turned toward him lifting his gun to fire when Benito fired; the bullet hit the man in the chest knocking him down.

When that happened, Tom stood up and fired, levered his rifle, and fired again. As he was doing it the third time I yelled, "Stop! Their hands are up!"

He turned toward me, the rifle cocked, and his eyes blazing. He was panting and I stood motionless lest he pull the trigger.

"Tom," I spoke softly. "What's wrong with you?"

He seemed to come to his senses, but didn't say anything. The wildness in his eyes was gone. He uncocked the rifle, turned and walked down the hill toward the campsite.

CHAPTER 23 – A Dark Night

When we walked into the camp Hidalgo was over talking to the teamsters; he had already disarmed the other guards. Two were dead and one badly wounded. Laying there groaning I could see he was bleeding severely from a wound just above his hip. The other guards just sat there with a sour look on their faces.

"Help him!" I ordered.

"*Por que?* He die anyway," said one. I don't ever recall ever seeing such a lack of caring for one's fellow man.

There was great agony etched on the face of the wounded man. I took a step toward him, and as I did his face darkened. His eyes opened wide with fear as his body stiffened and he screamed, "El Diablo!" and then his body relaxed, he was dead.

"I told you," said the one with the great apathy. It was all I could do to keep from smashing his face with the barrel of my rifle.

"Shame to die like that," I said to no one in particular.

Tom must have heard me for he questioned, "Why is it a shame?"

I turned to look at him. "To die without any hope. To die with fear tuggin' at your soul."

He looked a bit reflective with wrinkles forming on his

forehead then changed the subject. "We still have us a problem. Two of Ceron's men are alive. If you had let me shoot them we wouldn't be caught in a fix like this."

I went to one of the guards. "Get up!" He just looked at me so I prodded him in the back of the neck with my rifle. "I said, get up!"

Turning my attention back to Tom. "There he is, shoot him, but be sure you're lookin' him square in the eyes when you pull that trigger." Turning, I went over to talk with Hidalgo.

Behind me I heard a gruff, "Sit down," and I breathed a sigh of relief.

"These men are scared," Benito said referring to the teamsters. "If Ceron finds out what happened their families will be tortured and killed."

"Will they drive the wagons to the border?" I asked. "Go check, while I unlock the wagons and let the people out.

As soon as they were out some ran immediately to the wagons with the children. There was crying, hugging, and carrying on as mothers and children were reunited. Others were just staring, standing there as if in a daze wondering what had happened.

Too late, I saw the woman the guards had kept out, grab a rock and run up behind the guard. Lifting the rock above her head she brought it down and smashed the head of her tormentor. There was a sickening crack and he fell over; now only one guard was alive.

He jumped up and away. "Get her, crazy woman!"

Benito grabbed her and took the rock away. She slumped to the ground, sobbing. One of the ladies stooped down beside her and held her.

I went to a woman standing, watching what had happened. "What was that all about?"

She looked at me, where there had been hardness, her eyes were now moist with tears. "He took her baby. If the children are not old enough to work or not weaned they cannot be sold and are taken away."

"Taken?" I asked, not sure that I wanted an answer.

"Just taken away; done away with; killed; given to the..." then she broke down crying and ran off.

It was now dark and we had built up fires in front of the wagons. There was no food, and only the water in the barrels. One of the teamsters said they were to be resupplied at their stop tomorrow night.

"So you were to be gone, five, maybe six days?" I asked the driver who did most of the talking with Benito. "Then you really can't get back early.

"No, Senor, El Diablo would know something had happened."

Another teamster jumped to his feet. "He already knows!" he exclaimed with disgust. "Our wives, our children are already dead!"

"You don't know that," I countered.

Giving me a hard look, he said. "He has the Evil Eye, he knows!"

People had settled down by the fires. Tom had secured the only guard left, and came over to where Benito and I were standing.

"I reckon...."

"Butler! You have forgotten that I'm in charge, so you just quit your reckoning," said Tom hardening again.

I looked at Benito; he just shrugged as Tom continued. "The Mexicans could drive the women and children north to Eagle Pass and be back in the time allotted. Butler, you'll go with them while me and Hidalgo go back to the village."

"There is a problem," I began.

"You're right, and he's yours!" growled Tom. "You take care of him!"

I started to respond when Benito put his hand on my shoulder. Sighing, I then said. "When the guards don't return, what then? And you said Biggs was in town."

He made no comment, and turned toward the fire. Benito then spoke up. "Guess we'll figure it out when that time comes. Sleep, amigo; I'll stand guard."

I moved over to one of the wagons and grabbed a shovel. "The dead men; we better bury them first. They'll draw flies and other vermin."

CHAPTER 24 – Preparations

The next morning, after putting the coffee on, Benito told the teamsters of our plan. They were to drive the wagons to Eagle Pass; unless something went wrong they could make it in a couple of days. Then they could sneak back where Benito had their families.

It was after he finished explaining that he noticed, "Where is the sullen one?"

The teamsters looked at each other, questionly. Then one spoke up. "My sleep was disturbed when he got up last night, but I just thought it was the call of nature. I went back to sleep."

"Great!" muttered Tom in disgust.

Benito smiled and shrugged his shoulders. "So now, we just add another little problem."

Tom looked at him with disgust and threw the rest of his coffee in the fire where it sizzled. "This coffee is terrible!" Standing up he glared at both of us and walked away.

I went to one of the fires where there was another pot. Women, who wanted coffee, would come and take a sip from the pot or share from the few cups. By this time the other fires were out. There was nothing to cook, and the day was already warming up.

Going over to the woman I talked to last night, I

observed that she was a little disheveled, her hair was in tangles; but with some fixing up she could be a sightly woman. "Excuse me, ma'am," I began.

She looked my way. "Hannah, my name is Hannah, Mr. Ranger."

This was not the time fore me to be flustered around a woman. "Elias Butler. Ma'am, Hannah, we've got some problems."

She didn't smile, but there was a little quirk at the corner of her mouth.

"Do you know of anyone that can drive one of them wagons?"

"Yes, I can find someone. Go on."

"How many children are there without their mother or older sister?"

Her eyes seems to moisten. "Seven."

"Well," I removed my hat and brushed my hand over my hair. "I don't want to sound mean, but what shall we do with them? What wagon should they go in?"

She reached out and touched my hand. "I'll take care of it. Anything else?"

"Those wagons are closed in and stuffy. We have only the barrels of water on each wagon, and those have to last for at least two days." I paused and looked at her; she was waiting for me to continue. "It's gonna get hot. I figure that leavin' the back open would help some, but also, if the women wanted to walk they could, as long as they can keep up."

"That would help," she said.

"Well," I said, sort of stuttering. "We need to be on the road in the next twenty minutes. Tell the woman who will be drivin' I want her on the fourth wagon."

"We'll all be ready, Mr. Butler."

I went and grabbed the prisoner. As we walked by the

teamster that Benito and I had talked with, I stopped. "You have a name?" I asked and held out my hand.

"Roberto," he said shaking my hand.

"Roberto, I want you driving the third wagon. This..." and I jostled our prisoner, "will be your special baggage."

His eyes widened with a look of uncertainty. "Don't you fret none. He will be thoroughly secured."

As I was taking this low-life to the wagon the women and children were scurrying about and climbing into the wagons.

"Get up," I said.

He stood there, refusing. I drew my pistol and gave him a good thunk over his ear. "Get up," I said more forcefully. It seemed like he was still going to be stubborn, so I raised my pistol. He grabbed his ear with his tied hands, and then proceeded to climb up on the seat.

I made sure he was tied nice and tight. He began to let out a stream of cursing, some of it in English and some in Spanish. I didn't need a translator! Since I was up on the wagon seat I took out my pistol and whacked him over the other ear.

"Shut your mouth!" I ordered. "There are women and children here. Ifn I have any more trouble from you I'll gag you and tie you under the wagon."

That got his attention. Then he snarled, "El Diablo will make you suffer. He'll own your soul."

"Ha, I think you have more to fear from him than I do. And he can't have my soul as it already belongs to Jesus."

I could see he was ready to spout off again. "Nuh-uh," I said, raising my pistol. He sort of cringed, but didn't say anything.

Benito brought Fred up to me. I noticed Tom was already mounted. After handing me the reins Benito put his hand on my shoulder. "*Hermano*, I, too, have been reading the Book from which you read. This is what I read this morning. 'Teach me Thy way, O Lord, and lead me on a plain path, because of mine enemies.'" He pulled me close and embraced me. "I fear our enemies will keep us from seeing each other again." He broke away and not bothering using the stirrup, swung up into the saddle and galloped away.

I watched as he joined Tom and they returned up the arroyo the way we had come until finally their heads dipped below the rim. Fred snorted and brought me back to the present.

After I mounted, I pointed at the teamster in the lead wagon. "Let's go!"

He snapped the reins and they started out. I glanced at each wagon as it went by, nodding at each driver. When the fourth wagon came my way I got a surprise; it was Hannah at the reins. I rode up to her.

"Never driven a team of four horses," she said. "But I figured I could handle it."

I didn't say anything, just touched the brim of my hat in acknowledgement.

CHAPTER 25 – The Road to Eagle Pass

The day was quickly fulfilling its promise of being hot. The road was rough and dusty. By mid-morning most everyone was back riding in the wagons. It was stuffy, but it kept the intense heat radiating from the sun off of them.

Roberto said that this road would come to a fork about five miles from the village. That worried me a mite for a couple of reasons. It was too close to the village, anybody could be out riding and spot us.

Second, it meant we would have to spend extra time on the road, with a limited water supply. When we came to the fork we would have to travel in the dark to get sufficiently far enough away from the village.

I didn't want to stop, but knew we had to take a break. Each wagon carried two barrels of water. One for the occupants, and the other for the horses. Both needed to drink.

The teamsters took care of the horses and I went around and put a woman from each wagon in charge of a barrel. I rode Fred up and down the line; things were going smoothly.

"We've got to get back on the road!" I yelled. "Hurry!"

Some of the younger children were whimpering but even they sensed the importance of us to be back on the road. After checking with each of the ladies in charge it seemed like there was about half a barrel left on each wagon. That should be enough for us to make it, but we would be thirsty.

Riding by Roberto's wagon, he yelled down to me. "The prisoner, he says he is thirsty."

I had forgotten about him so I reached for my canteen to hand to Roberto. "Two swallows!"

"I can't hold it all tied up," he bellowed.

"Roberto, hold it for him; only two swallows!"

After receiving my canteen back I rode back to Hannah's wagon. "Doin' okay?" I asked.

"The horses do all the work," she replied. I touched the brim of my hat and rode out to the front.

It became my routine to scout ahead a few hundred yards, wait as the wagons passed me, then ride some more. This way Fred would not be pushed so hard.

We didn't stop at noon, except for a few minutes to give the horses a breather. There was no need to as we didn't have any food. That's when there began a small commotion.

"We need to stop, we need to drink," came the call. First from one wagon and then all began to join in the chorus.

I certainly could understand their complaint, but I also didn't want to stop this close to the village. It continued, "Stop! Stop!" I wondered if they yelled like that when they were being transported and guarded as slaves.

Riding to the lead wagon I put up my hand for him to halt. "Fifteen minutes, get a drink!" I only half-believed it would be fifteen minutes.

Down among the wagons there was some yelling and

screaming. I headed toward the sound. There was a scuffle between the keeper of the barrel and another woman. When I arrived at the wagon the woman I had put in charge was holding the side of her face. Two other women were restraining one holding the remains of a broken ladle in her hand. They all started to speak at once.

"Hold it!" I ordered.

Turning to the hurt woman, "What happened?"

"She wanted more than her share and wouldn't return the ladle after her turn. She tried to take more," pausing she removed her hand to show her split lip. "She broke the ladle when she hit me."

Tempers had simmered down a bit and the woman was released. She looked at me with contempt. "Who put you in charge anyhow?"

"I did," was my reply. "You don't have to travel with us." When I said that she must have realized I would leave her.

"How many of you didn't get a drink?" Four hands went up. "The rest of you load up; you four stay," and I rode to another wagon to fetch a dipping gourd.

Coming back I handed it to one of them. "Drink" and then to the driver. "Fall in at the end." Nudging Fred, he galloped up to the lead wagon and I told the teamster to move out.

The sun was just hanging above the horizon when we came to the fork. Riding next to the lead wagon I gave instructions. "Push the horses a little, but don't overdo it. We need to get eight to ten miles further today."

As each wagon passed, I hollered. "Keep up, don't lag behind!"

I lingered behind and walked Fred a ways down the road toward the village, perhaps fifty yards. The only tracks I saw were the wagons that came out yesterday and the footprints of a man staggering toward the village; the teamster that departed during the night.

I sat there pondering. Would he go straight to Ceron? He just might; he might figure that for his deed he would be rewarded, or at least pardoned. Hopefully, he would go check on his family first, and then sleep. He would be in rough shape. If he does the former I could expect some extra company later that night.

"Let's go, Fred," and I tugged on the reins turning him. It wasn't long before I caught up with the wagons. "We need to travel for a least two hours."

"The road, Senor, it is not good. It will be hard to see in the dark."

He was right. This was not much of a road. It had been traveled a few times, but there was little to distinguish it as a road. I kicked Fred and rode ahead for maybe a mile.

This was barren land, except to the east where the Rio flowed where there was green growth. Continuing on this road would bring us out north of Del Rio. I wanted to be shuck of them sooner; there had to be a place to cross south of Eagle Pass.

We would travel to just before dark; get camp set up. If El Diablo sent men, a few more miles wouldn't make much a difference. I prayed that there would be a way to cross the river.

Dismounting, I loosend the cinch to give Fred a little breather. Standing there looking at the road, then eastward, I pondered, prayed, and pondered some more. When I saw the wagons come in sight I tightened the cinch, mounted and rode back to them.

CHAPTER 26 – Night with the Women

We would be in a fix if Ceron sent men to attack as we only had three guns among us; the guard's pistol, mine, and my Henry. We traveled maybe eight miles before I called a halt while it was barely light. That would give the women time to gather up wood for fires and get a drink.

I directed us off the road, down toward the river a ways. Hopefully, there would be a place to cross if we continued this direction. I figured we had somewhere around fifteen more miles before we reached Eagle Pass. That may not sound like much, but traveling in these wagons over open land is slow going.

The night was still, almost too quiet. There was little talk and no gaiety around the fires that night, even among the children. Everyone was tired, and I knew how hungry they must be, but at least they had some water.

If Ceron was going to attack he would find us easily enough so I told them they could have fires, just keep them low. There was no need sending out an invitation, plus I didn't know of the Indian situation in the region either.

I found out the driver of the first wagon was Hector. Giving him the Henry, he would take first watch. Roberto came to me, and said he would take the second.

"You sure?" I asked. "You had to put up with our guest today."

"Si, he no problem. And Senor, our guest--he is a worried man. Worried that you keel him, or the El Diablo find and keel him. He is, what you might say, in a fix."

"What about you? Aren't you all in a fix?" I pointed to the teamsters.

"We will go back to get our families. Maybe we make it; maybe we die, but we must try," he paused. "We have no choice."

"Roberto, there is always a choice."

"No, Senor! There is not!" he said emphatically. "Not if you are a man! Not if you do what is right! There is only that way—no other! Call it destiny, call it fate, but it is the only way that must be taken."

I recalled my words to Tom. As men we had to do what was right.

"What about El Diablo?" I asked. "Do you believe he is the devil?"

"No, not the devil, but certainly a demon. He is evil and he has the 'evil eye.'"

"Do you really believe in that superstition?"

"You do too," he said point at my saddle. "You carry the stones."

I had forgotten about the bloodstones embedded in my saddle. Alejandro said they would guard against the "evil eye."

"Get some rest. Relieve Hector in three hours." Then I turned to walk down among the wagons.

I stopped at Roberto's wagon to check that our prisoner was secure. He was firmly tied to a wagon wheel, and Roberto was right, he wasn't as sullen as before.

"Did you get a drink?" I asked.

"Si," and that was all.

"Maybe you need a dose of hope."

"There is no hope. El Diablo is watching; I am a dead man." Then he looked up. "You are a dead man."

"Well, we all face it sometime. That's where the hope comes in, after death."

As I came to the next wagon I noticed the driver still sitting up on the seat. It was Hannah.

"Hannah, can I help you down?" There was no response. "Hannah!"

I don't know if she was asleep or just in a daze. She did reach her hand down and then sort of just fell. I had no choice but to catch her. She lingered just a bit in my arms then pulled away.

"One of the men helped with the horses. I was just too tired."

She fell back toward me, so naturally I had to catch her again. I looked around, hoping that no one was watching as I was a mite uncomfortable. I looked down at her and saw she was asleep, standing up. Reaching down I picked her up and then stooped so I could lay her down easier.

Her eyes opened, "Thank you, Elias." Then she rolled over on her side.

I finished my round and walked back up to the front. Knowing I should try to sleep I sat down by a wagon with my back against a wheel. No, there wouldn't be any sleep tonight.

Fred was saddled and I woke Hector. "Watch the last hour for me, and get everyone up the first sign of gray light. I'm going to scout ahead."

We moved slowly away from the camp going northeast toward the river. Sooner than I expected we came to the river. The stars were fast disappearing. From the looks of things we could enter here, but I couldn't see the other bank very well yet.

"Let's go, Fred, might as well get wet." I was hoping he could walk across. Entering the water it seemed to be swift, but not deep. We kept going, Fred was now walking in maybe only a foot of water. My eyes were searching the bank for a place suitable for the wagons.

Two-thirds of the way over, Fred plunged, losing his footing, Now swimming, but only for a few yards, and then he was walking again. The water was shallow and the bank an easy slope. He went up the incline and we were now in high grass and brush. If I remembered right, the road, was only a short distance away.

CHAPTER 27 – Moving Toward Freedom

I had been gone about an hour. The sun was peeking over the horizon with its promise of another sweltering day. The wagons were moving slowly, and for the most part in my direction.

Hector halted as I approached him. "Any problems getting started?" I asked.

"No, all are tired, but realize in a few hours this ordeal will be over."

"Good, angle down toward the way I came. Should come to the river in a couple of hours."

The wagons started to roll by. I noticed that Roberto had secured our prisoner. As the fourth wagon approached, there was Hannah, at the reins. I touched the brim of my hat as she went by and she gave a smile. There were a few walking, but everyone was keeping up with their wagon. As the last wagon passed, I gave a prayer of thankfulness. The men from El Diablo did not show.

Glancing at the back trail, I turned Fred and galloped back to the front. We were off the road so I needed to put my attention to getting the wagons to the river. The sun was now all alone up there in the sky, and the day was on its way to being hot.

There was a slight rise then a grade down to the place where we would cross. I was riding alongside Hector when from the rear of the caravan came screaming. Hector stopped. Kicking Fred, I rushed back.

As the last wagon came over the rise the right rear wheel had broken. One of the women was laying on the ground beside it holding her leg. Jumping off Fred I ran to her; the wagon hadn't fallen on her, thankfully. Upon closer inspection I saw that one of the spokes had flown from the broken wheel and hit her leg. I doubted that it was broken, but there would be quite the bruise.

The driver was already at the back helping the women and children out. As I approached I lifted my voice, "Anyone hurt?" There were some groans, but no one sounded out.

There were fourteen in the wagon plus the one laying injured on the ground. "A pair of you go to each of the other wagons." I looked at the driver. "Unhook the horses; we'll leave the wagon."

The injured woman was now sitting up, rubbing her leg as I turned back to her. "Here, let me help you stand."

I helped her up, and she could put some pressure on the leg, but couldn't take a step. I swooped her up and threw her on Fred, then took her to the last wagon.

"Take the door completely off," I told the driver. As he was working on that I picked her off my saddle and sat her down on the floor of the wagon, her legs dangling outside.

"Sorry, ma'am, best I can do for the time bein'."

There was a commotion coming from another wagon with quite a bit of yelling. I jumped on Fred and off we went to the middle of the wagons. Two women from the broken-down wagon were standing with hands on their hips. Another woman was crouching in the doorway.

I dismounted and one of the ladies standind said, "She won't let us in," pointing at the one in the door.

"Ain't no room for them; we're crowded as it is," argued the one protecting the entry. I noticed she held something in her hand as a weapon; the broken ladle. It was the same woman who caused the trouble at the water barrel.

I walked up to the wagon, reached and grabbed her arm and jerked her from the wagon. She landed on the hard dirt with a thud. I peered in the wagon. "Ladies, scrunch over some." Then nodded at the two standing outside. "There's room now."

Mounting Fred again, I was going to see if the driver could take over for Hannah.

"What about me?" whined the woman laying on the ground.

"Lay there, go back to Mal de Ojo, or walk, but you'll not cause any more trouble!" Jerking the reins on Fred I rode to Hannah's wagon.

"How're you doin'?" I asked.

"I'm making it fine," she paused. "You were kind of harsh back there, Ranger Butler."

I rubbed my chin which was now rough with whiskers. "Maybe, but you're a Texan--this is a hard land." I looked back toward the troublemaker, and the woman was now standing. "I have someone to take over for you if you want, Hannah"

"You don't think I can handle the job?" she questioned.

"Didn't say that. You've done right well. I said, if you wanted."

"My arms could use a little rest. As long as I can still sit up here."

I pointed at the driver and he climbed up. Hannah

relinquished the reins to him, then gave me a little smile. I gave Fred a nudge and we galloped back to the front.

"Let's get 'em movin', Hector. Just follow me. It's downhill to the river."

For the next couple of hours we moved slow and easy, following the slope downward. Finally, there it was the-- Rio Grande and on the other side, Texas.

The wagons stopped and I rode back telling all the teamsters to meet me at the river. I was a bit amused as I watched them all down to the edge of the water and splashing water on themselves.

"Ahhh, the Rio Bravo is so refreshing," exclaimed Roberto. I had forgotten that was the name those in Mexico called the Rio Grande.

I explained the situation, and then asked for suggestions. "Senor," spoke up Hector. "The wagons are loaded making them more heavy. Wouldn't it be better to get the women and children across?"

He was right. Now, how?

"Is there any rope?" I asked. I quit carrying one since I'd joined the Rangers.

From the driver of the wagon that broke down, "We have the reins from that team." He ran to get them.

Hector spoke up again. "Let me drive my wagon over to the shallows. We can tie the reins to it. Then Juan's wagon can go and sit in the river and we tie off to it. We need only about twenty feet you said."

"Let's get to it!"

The first wagon was unloaded and Hector was ready. I nodded and pointed. "Yeehaw! Yhaw! Yhaw!" Hector yelled, as he slashed the reins and the team hit the water at a near run. It was going well, then the horses hit the deep water, but their powerful legs pulled them up on the shallows. It looked as if the wagon might float, pulling the horses with it, but Hector yelled again and the horses moved forward and with them the wagon.

"Ready, Juan? Stop your horses shy of that deep water."

He went across with no problem. Now, the women and children. Right at the beginning was the strong current but the water was only about mid-thigh and eight feet across. Fred and I would carry the children and the smaller women.

Juan yelled that the lines were secure. "Okay," I began to give instructions. "This first section is swift, but not deep, just go slow, and keep your footing. Then when you get to where Juan is, wait by the wagon until I get there, then you can begin to cross the deep section. Grab the reins that are stretched. When you have no more footing, use the reins and pull yourself to the other side."

They were a little tentative, but once the first few crossed there were no problems. Roberto went first to show them how to hold onto the reins and then stayed to help Hector pull them up out of the water. Thank the Lord there were no mishaps, and Fred only had to carry children across three times.

Now, the wagons. I rode to Hannah's. "Your choice."

She straightened her shoulders, "I'll ride."

Roberto was back over and climbing aboard his wagon. Hector had driven his up through the low brush and Juan had followed. The river was now clear.

"Hey! What about me?" Our prisoner spoke up.

I looked at him. "Better hope that your wagon doesn't tip over." With that Roberto snapped the reins and in they plunged.

As Hannah's wagon approached I touched the brim of my hat and off they went. Four across, three left to go. Number 5, then 6, no problems. Now the last wagon.

Going to the back I asked the lady with the hurt leg. "Want to ride with me or stay in the wagon?"

"I'll go with the wagon."

They hit the deep water fine, but when the horses came to the shallows they stumbled. The other trips had worn away the river bottom, and they were struggling to gain a foothold. As the wagon was began to tip and fill with water, the woman fell out.

As she was splashing around, Fred took off toward her. "Swim!" I yelled. "It's not far!"

I don't know if she didn't hear me or her leg hurt too much to kick, or if she even knew how to swim. But Fred knew exactly what to do, as we had crossed many rivers while taking steers to Kansas. I was able to reach down and grab her arm pulling her up partially on the saddle. Then we dropped her safely on the other side.

The teamster had worked those horses so that the wagon didn't tip, now he had them up on the bank. What a day! I looked back to the other side and there stood that cantankerous woman.

I sighed, "Let's go, Fred."

She was standing there, frightened. I held out my arm; she grabbed it and I swung her up behind me. "Just hang on."

CHAPTER 28 – A New Name, a New Life

"Thank you," she said softly as Fred moved up the bank on the Texas side of the Rio.

As I dropped her off, her arm lingered on my leg. "Please, I'm sorry."

Looking down from where I was mounted I saw a woman transformed from a sullen, angry form of her species into a humble, winsome-looking lady. "We all have our times," I responded.

"I was scared; I am scared." She stopped and pointed toward the rest of the women, some walking around, others laying in the tall grass. "We have lost everything: homes, families, husbands, some have lost children...." she started to cry and moved away.

This land was rugged and tough on a woman. How much tougher would it be now for them? They'd make it, most of them anyway, and Texas would be stronger because of the likes of them.

Giving Fred a little kick, I rode to the center of the throng of women. "Let's not linger! We need to get movin'; only a few hours left." There was some murmuring, but everyone started to pull themselves together.

"You drivers, check your wagons and move to the road," I yelled pointing. "You're only about thirty yards away. We'll load when you're on the road.

It wasn't long before Hector had his team ready. I rode in front of his horses and he drove carefully over the grass and small brush. When he saw the road he broke out into a smile and snapped his reins. "*Amigo!*"

"Move on up the road, and get your people loaded."

Soon all the wagons were on the road and the women and children were piling in. I spotted the woman I had carried across the river walking toward the back of the last wagon. Riding to her, I put down my arm and swooped her up.

Taking her to the last wagon, I said, "Ride up here," and off I went.

Upon reaching the third wagon I yelled up at Roberto. "Untie him and throw me his gun."

I caught it as he tossed it to me, and spun the cylinder. The prisoner's eyes followed as I cocked and uncocked his pistol. Opening the cylinder, I removed the bullets and gave the gun back to him.

"What's your name?" I asked.

"Tomas de la Fuente."

"Well, it's Tom Franks now. You had no hope, now you do. Texas is a big land. For that matter, the West is vast and needs men with hope."

He reached down his hand. "*Gracias.*"

I shook it and in the palm of my hand was a double-eagle. "All I can spare," I said. "Take one of the extra horses. I know there's no saddle; get a honest job and buy one. Also, get rid of those Mexican spurs, most Texas boys don't like them."

I started to turn Fred, but held him for another

minute. "You might want to ride on to Del Rio. There's a chance King Fisher might know you."

"Why you do this?"

"Just figured you would take advantage of a second chance in life. A man on a cross centuries ago died for me to give me a second chance."

I rode up to Hector. He was ready to go, sitting there on the wagon seat with his hands full of reins. "In Eagle Pass, next to the hotel, is a cantina. Go inside and ask politely for King Fisher. He'll help you. Tell him, Elias Butler sent you."

"*Vaya con Dios,*" he snapped the reins, starting his team.

"I'll see you in a couple of days. Let's go, Fred," and we started back down the row of wagons.

Then I saw her, standing there. Halting Fred, I dismounted.

"Hannah, can I give you a hand?"

"This is it, isn't it?" she asked.

I wasn't real sure what she was meaning until she spoke again. "I'll never see you again."

"Well, ah...."

"Don't say anything," and she came to me and gave me a hug. Releasing me she turned and I helped her up on the seat.

"Elias, if you decide to come calling, please change your shirt. You smell to high-heaven," and then turned her head looking straight forward.

Mounting, I settled down in the saddle. The wagons were moving by as I looked down at my shirt. "That night," I thought to myself, "now seemed so long ago."

Dismounting, I untied my bag. There was my dress shirt. Reckon it wouldn't stay white long, but Hannah was right, I smelled rank.

I wadded up the shirt and threw it in the brush. I took my knife and cut the waist of my undershirt and tore it off and threw it along with the foul shirt. Putting on my dress white shirt, I felt half-naked without an undershirt.

As I mounted, my hand touched one of the bloodstones. "Okay, Lord," I prayed. "Let's see what's waiting for me in Mal de Ojo."

I nudged Fred into a trot, which he held for maybe twenty yards. Then, perhaps sensing something, went into a gallop and soon into a full-fledged run.

CHAPTER 29 – Lorenzo

The sun was dipping towards its evening resting place when I rode into the village with no name. Going straight to the small corral, I dismounted then led Fred to the water trough. The kid must have heard me ride up.

"Senor," he said greeting me and walking out of the little barn. I unsaddled Fred and tossed the saddle on the top rail of the corral, and set my gear beside the post. I took the Henry with me.

"Brush and feed him," I said.

"Si, Senor, two-bits," he replied with a grin.

I flipped him a quarter and started toward the dingy cantina, but stopped and turned back toward the kid. "Chico? What name were you given?"

"Lorenzo!" he declared.

"My, that's a man's name. You better start growin' into it. Take good care of my horse."

He jerked his shoulders back, and I think he might have grown three inches just standing there. Smiling I turned back toward the cantina and entered.

"Tequila?" asked the proprietor.

"No, no, coffee and some frijoles, *por favor.*"

I had been sitting only a few minutes when a hefty

woman from the back corner brought my plate of beans and a couple of them tortillas. She went over to the small counter for the coffee and a cup. After she poured it I reached for the handle on the cup and took a sip. It was almost like syrup and very bitter. Probably the worst coffee I'd ever tasted, but better than no coffee.

I finished the cup and plate of beans right quick. She smiled and rushed me a refill of both.

"Lorenzo your son?" I asked.

She smiled proudly. "Si."

"He's gonna make a good man." I don't know if she understood or if she thought I was asking for more coffee as she topped off my cup.

I sat there for a spell pondering the situation that lay before me. There were maybe two, three hours of light left. I didn't know what I could do in Mal de Ojo during the night. Where Benito and Tom were I had no idea. They would have to find me.

A sound began to filter through the room. "Is that music?" I asked the proprietor.

"Si," he answered in a distant voice. "Evil music to prepare for the big day tomorrow."

"Fiesta of some sort?"

"Fiesta of death. Tomorrow some will die. Tonight, El Diablo will celebrate."

"Maybe I'll go over and have a look-see."

"Senor," he said placing his hand on my arm. "Do not go. There is nothing but wickedness tonight. Stay here, help us in case the evil demons come our way."

I was right curious about the goin's-on, but he made sense and I definitely needed some sleep. I could wait until this "fiesta of death" took place tomorrow.

Walking out of the cantina, I went to get my bedroll. Lorenzo was standing there, looking across the river toward the sound—mesmerized. The first thing that entered my mind as he stood there was the "evil eye."

He didn't hear me approach. "Kinda gets to yuh." When I spoke he jumped. "If you're gonna survive in this land, always be aware of what's goin' on around you."

I could tell he was embarrassed that he didn't hear me approach. Reaching down, I gave him a moment to recover, and collected my gear. "Mind if I sleep in the hay tonight?" Then as I walked by him I tucked the Henry under my arm and placed my hand on his shoulder. "Lorenzo," he looked at me. "It doesn't pay to get involved with the devil's play."

He didn't say anything so I continued to the barn. Laying my bedroll down on the hay, my mind returned to the time when Walker, my brother, and I left Tennessee and all the nights I slept on the hay in a livery.

When I woke the next morning there was a strange stillness. As I tugged on my boots, I thought to myself that I must have really been tired as I slept through all the noise of the celebration across the Rio. Sitting there I checked the action on the Henry. Then I unloaded my pistol, cleaned it and wiped it down as well as the bullets, then reloaded.

Standing, I stretched and Lorenzo ran in, "Senor, mama, has breakfast for you." Carrying the Henry with me I put one hand on his shoulder as we walked together to the cantina.

I went in and as soon as my legs were under the table coffee was brought to me. It was about the same as last night only not quite so thick.

Then from the corner came Lorenzo's mother. She was carrying a plate which she set in front of me. "For you, Senor."

There were three tiny eggs; they must have had some

pullets running around somewhere. The eggs were sitting on top of beans and covered with peppers. Next to it was some kind of sausage.

It greatly humbled me. This was a meal they had probably never made for themselves. My mercy, eggs! Even if they were small that was a rarity out here. I took a sip of coffee, then bowed my head. As I raised it, and picked up the fork to take a bite, the words of King Fisher came to me-- "last meal." If that be so, I was going to enjoy it.

There was no need for me to hurry. With the celebration last night I didn't think the folks of Mal de Ojo would wake up much before noon.

After finishing, I stood and went to speak to Lorenzo's mother. "Mamacita, you're an angel." She looked at me and began to cry. She brought her dress up to wipe her eyes and turned away.

That sort of stunned me so I walked to the door and out to saddle Fred. I saw at a glance that he was saddled and all my gear was tied on. I checked to see if everything was tied tight, and then pulled on the cinch.

Lorenzo and his father stood there silently as I mounted. When I looked at them the elder gave the sign of the cross. There was no need for any words, but I didn't relish the idea that they thought I was going to meet my Maker today.

One more stop to retrieve my cache of bullets and the dynamite. Uncovering it I put six sticks of the dynamite in my shirt and the rest in my saddlebags. I filled my pockets with bullets and included the rest of the boxes in the bags with the dynamite. Mounting and settling down in the saddle, I clicked my tongue. "Let's go, Fred, and see what kinda day the Lord has prepared for us."

CHAPTER 30 – Torture in Mal de Ojo

The Rio Grande flowed on toward its final destination in the Gulf of Mexico. It was a process that never ceased. I took one backward glance at it as Fred topped the sloping hill. There in front of me lay Mal de Ojo, a place in the passage of time.

I allowed Fred to take his time as he walked the road toward our fate. I rode to the side of the first building, keeping out of sight, where I dismounted. I didn't loosen the cinch for I didn't know if I would have to leave in a hurry or not. Rummaging through my saddlebags I found the box of matches. I took a small handful and stuffed them in the top left pocket.

Stepping up on the boardwalk, I moved leisurely, not wanting to draw attention to myself. A crowd was starting to gather toward the end of the village by the fountain.

As I passed by a ramshackle cantina, a man burst from the building bumping into me. "Sorry, Senor. El Diablo has summoned the entire village."

As I continued my walk, I observed villagers racing toward the fountain area. It wasn't until I was at the corner of Ignacious' place did I see the sight—three men, tied to X-shaped crosses: Tom, Benito, and the teamster that fled the camp. Sitting on the ground below him was a woman and four children.

I felt conspicuous in my white shirt. I shouldn't have been so concerned as most of the men were wearing white shirts, but I pushed myself as close as I could to the wall of the cantina. I stayed back from the main entrance as I remembered Ignacious and his shotgun.

There was the sound of a trumpet, and the the music of guitars. Two brightly dressed young women came from the fountain area dancing to the music, their skirts swirling high on their legs. One was dressed in red, the other in black. As they were dancing one of the giant guards moved to stand behind the tied teamster.

The music stopped as quickly as it had started. There was an eerie silence, and then, he appeared, Markel Ceron—El Diablo. Close behind him was the other giant guard.

Oh, my mercy, did he make a show. Prancing to the center, wearing the same black outfit and red sash I last saw him in, with high, black-polished riding boots. However, this time he was wearing a black gunbelt adorned with silver conchos. The butt of the gun was bright white, I figured ivory or pearl. He then waved his hand from side to side and as he did the people gave a bow. I wasn't about to bow, so I just stooped down staying lower than those in front of me.

"My people," he said raising his voice. "This is a momentous and fortunate day for Mal de Ojo. Three have been caught trying to do harm to the village and undermine the established government. Two of these men were actually here living among us, and one recently in my employ.

He proceeded to the center post. Halting, he reached for a pair of black gloves and put them on. With one hand he took hold of the man's jaw.

"Ricardo, why? Why have you brought this upon yourself," he paused and looked down at the little family, "and upon those you love?"

El Diablo reached down and took the arm of Ricardo's wife. "Stand up!" She stood, weeping.

"Ricardo Sandoval, you have been found guilty of conspiracy against the people of Mal de Ojo." Then a little softer. "You should have first come to me and told me of the attack, rather than to your family."

He nodded at the big guard who had something in his hand. El Diablo put pressure on the jaw, Ricardo's mouth opened and the guard thrust the hook in his mouth. In seconds, he pulled Ricardo's tongue out, and reached with his other hand for a dagger. El Diablo released his hand and stepped back. The knife flashed, slicing the tongue off, one piece held in the hook. Blood gushed from the victim's mouth.

Looking back at the woman, El Diablo ordered. "Put out your hands!" She refused. He grabbed her by the elbow and twisted. I could see her wince in pain. "Put out your hands!"

Now crying, she lifted her arms and opened her hands. "Take it, or the same will happen to your son!" She reached out and the giant placed the bloody tongue in them. "A memorial for you," he sneered.

Turning back to the bleeding victim. "Ricardo Sandoval, you have been found guilty of treason against the rule of El Diablo." He nodded at the guard again and the dagger slashed the throat of the one-time teamster. His head slumped forward and in seconds he was dead.

"A terrible judgment, but a lesson for all!" came the voice of El Diablo. As he lifted both arms high, a cheer rose from the crowd.

My mind was swirling. These people were plumb loco. Then he was speaking again, "Bring out what else we have uncovered."

From behind the fountain on the market side came guards leading seven women, and two younger girls, all tied on a rope. "There," spoke El Diablo pointing. "Are the wives and two children of the men who turned against your village. They will take the place of those who were stolen from our midst."

Then he pointed at the wife of Sandoval. "You will join them!" She stood there in shock until pushed by the large guard. Another shove and she headed to them, still holding the dripping tongue.

Looking down he pointed at one of the children, a young girl. "You! Go with her!"

He motioned for the guard to take away the other three children.

Edging up to a man standing to the side of me. "What of the small children?"

He waved as if to tell me to go away, but then said very softly. "You do not want to know."

CHAPTER 31 – Two Men on Crosses

"This man," said El Diablo walking toward Tom, "was sent as a spy."

He stopped and began glancing at the crowd. Tom was not far from where I was standing. "A spy, as well as that man," he turned and pointed at Benito.

Stepping close to Tom, El Diablo again began looking through the crowd on my side. I moved close to a man with a white shirt, and was also partially hidden by a post. I could almost feel his eyes probing, seeking me out; I dared not look his way lest our eyes meet.

El Diablo reached up. I held my breath thinking he was planning to do the same to Tom as he did to Sandoval, but instead he placed his gloved hand flat against Tom's shoulder.

"Spies caught are normally executed, but he is a Texas Ranger." He stopped and motioned for someone to join him. "We were fortunate to have this brave man come to our aid and betray him and his friends."

The man from the crowd walked up and stood in front of El Diablo. It was Biggs. El Diablo took his hand from Tom and placed it around the shoulder of Biggs. "It takes a brave man to betray his friends; those who seek to do wrong to the people of Mexico."

"Go ahead, Mordo," and the giant guard reached up and tore the shirt off Tom.

"This brave man told us of a Captain McNelly," started El Diablo again, "who is seeking to destroy our good friend Cortinas to the south. These were sent to spy on us. Then the Rangers could come and destroy us."

"Do not be afraid! This will not happen for you are protected by El Diablo!" He thumped his fist against his chest. "There is one left to be found," and his eyes roamed through the crowd again. "Soon he will be in our clutches as well."

"Mordo, prepare this prisoner as our new friend helps us." El Diablo said, stepping away from Tom as the great giant guard, Mordo, took out his dagger.

"Gringo, to show the grace of El Diablo, not to you but to our friends the Americanos, you will not be killed. As you are a spy I have every right to do so. However, I do want to leave you a momento of El Diablo's grace."

With that, the giant cut a large X across the chest of Tom. The lines were about a half-inch wide. Taking the dagger, he dug a little deeper into one corner. At that time I noticed he still held the hook. Firmly attaching the hook to the piece of skin that was cut he left it dangling.

"Pull it," ordered El Diablo, staring into the eyes of Biggs. "Show everyone you now belong to El Diablo."

Tentatively at first he grabbed the hook and started to pull. Nothing, only a howl from Tom. "Pull!" screamed El Diablo and Biggs yanked as hard as he could. Even from where I was standing I could hear the skin rip, and then the bloodcurdling yell from Tom. Biggs held the hook with a long strap of skin.

The pain had been too much for Tom for he passed

out. It was just as well as Biggs tore the other strip off. Mordo had went for a bucket of water.

"Wake him up," came the order from El Diablo.

Tom's eyes were dazed, but he was now conscious. "Look at me, Ranger. Your life has been spared by me, El Diablo. If the infection sets in, that is not my doing. Never come back to Mexico!" Looking at Mordo. "Finish the job! Make sure he doesn't bleed to death and send him back across the Rio Bravo."

El Diablo walked away and toward Benito. I watched, almost in a daze myself. Mordo grabbed the right thumb of Tom. He began to pull. I heard the crack, then break. Mordo reached up with both hand and ripped Tom's thumb off. He quickly tied the arm with rawhide as a tourniquet. I hadn't noticed but another man had brought up Tom's horse, and also held a pouch of something.

Mordo reaching in the pouch and took a handful of the substance and poured it into each side of the X. He went to a man in the crowd and took his cigar. Touching the lighted end to the X there was a quick flare and the smell of burning flesh. Gunpowder. At least it cauterized the wound.

Tom was totally unconcious now as he was tied belly-down on his horse. "Take him to the river. Whip the horse across if you need to," ordered Mordo to the man. Then he walked to join El Diablo.

That devil-man was standing in front of Benito. "Look in my eyes, you Ranger scum. Look, so I can own your soul before you die!"

Benito, who had already been stripped, lifted his head and gazed into the eyes of El Diablo. "You can't control me!" and spit into the eyes of El Diablo.

Foaming with rage, El Diablo began to curse and started raining blows upon Benito with his fists. Finally, after several blows, he settled down. "We shall see, Ranger!"

El Diablo raised his hands and waved to someone. "Let the pigs out!"

From a pen somewhere behind the market came a host of pigs. My mind immediately thought, "Legion."

There was quiet, even the snorting of the pigs seem to stop as Benito spoke calmly. *"Dios, en tus manos encomiendo mi espiritu."*

That seemed to enrage El Diablo even more for he took the dagger from Mordo and slit the lower belly of Benito for the pigs to feed on as the entrails fell out.

"No!" I screamed.

I pushed through the crowd, drew my pistol, and shot my friend, Benito through the head. I fired at the pigs hoping they would feed upon those wounded or killed. Catching a glimpse of El Diablo running, I snapped a shot at him, missing. Now there was pandemonium.

CHAPTER 32 – Death and Destruction

"Biggs!" I hollered. He was standing not fifteen feet from me.

I lifted my pistol, he drew, and we both fired. My shot hit him. As he was trying to lift his gun for another shot I fired into him the second time. He fell to the ground laying in the dirt mixed with the blood of Tom Brown.

Stepping back against the post, I began to reload and let the empty brass cases fall to the ground. I looked around to gain my bearings, then headed toward El Diablo's office.

Upon entering I saw him standing in front of his desk. "Ceron, you're nothin' but a lunatic!"

"Ceron was my name given on this earth, but my true identity is El Diablo!" he snarled. "Today, Butler, you will belong to me."

"'Fraid not," I took a step to the right as I had done with Salas and drew. I wasn't going to give him an edge.

He was fast! Even as my gun was clearing the holster, he fired. I felt the bullet hit me high on the left shoulder, twisting me slightly. My bullet found its mark, high on his chest, but dead center; it had to have shattered his breast-bone.

I fired a second shot, this time hitting him low, in the belly. He fired, but his bullet hit the floor a few feet in front of me. His eyes were wide in surprise, and I expected also in pain. He staggered toward the well and threw one leg over the opening.

As I started to walk toward him, he tried to lift his gun to fire, but couldn't and it tumbled to the floor. "I am El Diablo," he said trying to raise his voice, but the words came out in a choking sound. "I will be back, I will haunt you," and he flung himself to the side and into the well. I heard the sound of rattles, then one last scream.

I was standing by the desk surveying the room wondering what happened to the two giant guards. That was quickly answered with a shot that shattered the lamp sitting on the desk next to my left arm. The kerosene spilled on the desk and onto the floor followed by the flames.

The giant guard was running toward me and fired again. I dropped to the floor close to the desk, but away from the flames. Raising up I fired hitting him in the hip. He stumbled and fell, his gun clattering as he hit the floor. I saw a hand reach to the top of the dry well and he pulled himself up.

The guard called Mordo, came in from the far side and rushed to his friend. He didn't seem to have a gun. Enough of this! I reached inside my shirt and pulled out two sticks of the dynamite. I lit one and threw it over Mordo's head.

He gazed at it; then realizing what it was, he began to scramble on his knees toward the back leaving his friend behind. Lighting the other I threw it in the snake pit. Hesitating, the thought struck me that I'd better be getting out.

I sprinted out the way I had come. As I hit the

boardwalk just outside, the blast knocked me off my feet. It was soon followed by the second blast. The building was crumbling and the fire was beginning to consume it. I crawled up close to the fountain. Removing the the empty cartridge cases, I reloaded.

The cantina was next, then to find the prisoners. Standing up I took a step toward it when I heard. "Hombre." It was the guard who had sat next to me during my trial.

He was there, ready for me. "It doesn't have to be this way," I said. "You can walk away."

"I have no choice. I am Merkel's brother," and he drew. His bullet did not seem close to hitting me, but mine hit him in the chest.

He fell, clutching at his heart. "Gracias, Hombre." I turned toward the cantina, and not two feet from me was a large, dead rattlesnake. It had been ready to strike me; his bullet had been aimed at the snake.

No time to dwell on it. A drop of blood fell on my hand; no time to dwell on that either. I walked into the cantina, took a couple of steps to my right and shot into the corner. I saw movement behind the counter. "Ignacious, don't touch the shotgun!" He backed away as my gun was pointed at him.

There were maybe half dozen men in there; funny, they wanted to know what was going on as they were standing in the middle of the room, but didn't want to get close enough to find out.

I stepped to the table where I had eaten a few days before; there was a candle burning. "Is there a back way out of here?" I asked, as I reached in my shirt for another stick of dynamite. "If so, I'd find it now." I lit the dynamite and they all started for the back door at the same time.

Throwing the stick to the far end of the counter I ran

out. Seconds later, Ignacious followed limping, "Senor," he cried. "The snake--it was not dead."

Then the blast came, blowing his little world to bits. He just sat there in the street. I looked at him and saw he was bleeding just above his right ankle. "No time. Go to the river." I left him still sitting there.

I now started toward the market trying not to look at the form of Benito. I had to find the women and children. Several villagers were hiding in the market, behind and under the tables of produce. "If you want to live, get out!" I yelled.

Going on through to where I had seen the guards bring the women, I was hoping to find where they went. As I stepped out the other side, a bullet struck the post on my right. I returned fire blindly, and ducked back inside the darkness of the market.

I searched for the shooter, but could not see anyone. Then from my left, a man ran. It was one of the guards of the women. I fired, missed, and fired again. The man stumbled and fell to his knees, but was up quickly and running again. I fired once more as he dove into the doorway of the two-story building. If the captives were in there, I'd never get them out.

CHAPTER 33 – Release

I dropped back to the market. The people had left except for one man scrounging around. "You!" I yelled. He started to run. "Stop!" He did, and when he turned I motioned him over to me.

I had to do something about the bleedng before I lost too much blood. When the villager came to where I was standing I turned the back of my shoulder to him. "Is it bleedin'?" I asked.

"Si, Senor."

Looking at the tables I saw some scarves. "Grab a couple of those and put some pressure on the wounds." Then I began to look around for something to hold the bandages in place.

"How about this?" he asked holding up some twine. It looked as if it were some kind of reed woven together. Grabbing several of them he wrapped them under my arms.

"Tie them tight over the bandage in the back. I must really look a sight. My good white, dress shirt, dirty and blood-soaked with a bright green and blue scarf all wrapped up in twine.

He started to leave. "Hold on!" I grabbed him. "Where are the women and children? Are they in the large buildin'?"

Dropping his head slightly, he then answered. "I don't know."

I cocked the pistol and put it in his face, "*Senor, por favor El Diablo?*"

"He's dead," I said matter of factly. "Want to join him?"

He was shocked I could tell. I didn't know if it was my threat or the news about El Diablo. I asked again. "Are they in the two-story buildin'?"

Walking to the back of the market, he started to step out, when my hand clinched the back on his shirt. "Not a good idea. Just tell me."

From inside the market area, he pointed to the left. "There is a building to the left, near the corral and pig pens. They are there, I think."

"Get!" and I turned toward the opening. I saw the building he was talking about. It looked at if it was used for a livery or place where they stored feed.

It was all open space up to the building. I knew there were probably two guards, maybe more. It wasn't doing me any good standing where I was, so taking a deep breath I hustled to the left corner of the building. No shots.

That little run left me weak. I took a moment to catch my breath, but I couldn't worry about my condition. Some how I had to get the guards outside. It would be too dangerous for those inside if I just busted on through the door.

Seeing a piece of wood nearby, I picked it up and started banging against the side of the building. It was only a minute or so until I heard the door open. After banging a few more times I jumped around the corner. The man was surprised, and hesitated just enough that I was able to get two shots off, both hitting him.

I hadn't reloaded when I was in the market, so I ducked back behind the corner of the building to do so. Hearing a commotion, I peered around. The other guard was out on the ground with two women on him, beating him. Another woman rushed out and picked up the gun of the fallen guard.

"Get off him," she hollered at the women.

As they got up, he rolled over quickly. She fired and missed; he fired hitting one of the women. The one with the gun fired again, this time hitting him in the head. He went limp.

I started toward them, and she turned my way, pointing the gun. "No! No! I'm a Ranger! I'm here to help!"

She lowered her arms, but kept a tight grip on the gun. The woman who had been shot was being tended by her companion. There was quite a bit of blood, but upon examination I saw that the bullet just grazed her in the side.

Going to the one with the gun, "Get the women and children across the river, pronto! The village is on fire. Hurry!"

She gave me a questioning look. I repeated, "Don't hesitate. Go. Your men will be coming from over there."

By that time, the other women were standing at the doorway. "Go! Go!" I yelled again. They scurried back inside to gather the children, then all ran out.

I watched them enter the market place, then reached for a stick of dynamite. Pulling a match from my pocket I flicked it with my thumbnail striking it to a flame. Lighting the fuse I threw it into the building then ran to the market.

Seconds later the explosion shattered the building.

Looking back into the market I saw a lamp. I wrapped my hand around the base and lifted the chimney, then lit with wick. After replacing the chimney I went toward the demolished building and heaved the lamp. Upon hitting the wreckage it burst into flame. Now on to the large, two-story building.

The alcalde's office and El Diablo's quarters were ablaze and the flames were moving toward the market. The thought of the flames of hell flittered through my mind, but this was no time for pondering. I rushed to the side of the building and then to the back. Looking up I saw the slits that were windows. Lighting the fuse of another stick of dynamite I reached up and tossed it into the cell and ran for cover diving around the front of the building.

The impact jarred my wounded shoulder, but I didn't dwell on the pain as there the explosion followed. As soon as that happened I rushed to the front doorway. I was hoping if that there were any guards they would be hunkered down, trying to cover themselves. Lighting the fuse on the final stick, I opened the door, threw it in, and started to run for the market.

Then I was hit, and caught up in massive arms. They encompassed me and began squeezing. The pain in my shoulder was excruciating. I noticed that one of the arms around me was blackened, the flesh badly burned. Mordo had somehow survived.

My arms were pinned to the side, thus making me unable to get to my gun. But with my arms under his it took more effort on his part to squeeze my chest. Sooner or later I knew that my bones would begin to crack. Then an explosion threw us both to the ground, loosening his grip.

Mordo was up before me, reaching for his dagger. His

face and right side of his body were badly burned, in some places the flesh completely burned off. Now, he was burning inside with desire to kill me. It would be over in seconds, the dagger in hand, he lunged for me. I recovered in time to draw my pistol and fire. I knew one shot would not stop him.

His arm came up to drive the dagger down into me. I emptied the cylinder, firing as fast as I could into his body. The bullets hit, driving him back slightly. He made a final, death plunge at me, the knife coming down, but falling short his effort drove the knife into the earth.

Quickly, I reloaded and looked around. I wondered if there were anymore guards willing to fight.

CHAPTER 34 – Evil...Ashes

My body was hurting as I walked back through the market and into the little square. I could feel the heat coming from my left from the burning buildings. As I walked past, I avoided looking at the body of Benito, but noticed one of the women with her children. The wife of Ricardo was trying to get his body off the cross.

Seeing them struggling, I walked over to help. I couldn't find my jackknife so I went to the body of the brother of El Diablo and took the knife off his belt. Going back, I started to cut the rawhide strips.

"No," said his wife taking the knife. "Let me."

I went to the front to hold the body so that when he was freed I could lower him to the ground. Looking at the young boy I said, "Go find some horses."

He just looked at me. *"Dos caballos! Andele!"* said his mother.

After Ricardo's bonds were cut he fell slightly toward me as I held him. I gently laid him down and walked to get Fred. The fire was now beginning to ignite the last building on that side. Fred was waiting behind that building.

Instead of mounting, I walked him over to Benito. The woman saw me, and came over to begin cutting his bonds. I held the man, my friend ... the man I had killed. When he was released, I carefully lowered his body to the ground.

I went again to Ceron's brother and seized the sash he was wearing. Taking it back to the body of Benito, I bound up his slashed belly. By that time the young boy was there with the horses.

Carefully, making sure the sash was bound tightly, I picked up my friend's body and draped it over the horse. Taking the pieces of rawhide I secured his body on the back of the horse. I would take him across the Rio Grande to bury him in Texas.

I went over to Ricardo's wife. "Where do you want him buried?"

"Not here," she murmured. "This place is evil. He is dead, it will not matter to him, but I do not want him here."

I nodded, then with the woman's help I lifted her dead husband over the back of the horse, and tied him down. We started walking toward the river. When we arrived at the edge of the bank, I mounted Fred. Holding the reins in my left hand, I grabbed the boy and swung him up behind me and then changing the reins to my right, entered the river.

The water had gone down, and was now only to the top of the front knees of Fred. The current was almost negligible. The boy jumped down when we reached the other side, and I went back for the two smaller children.

"Put the older one behind me, and then hand me the younger child in my right arm."

I held the reins in my left hand, "Easy, Fred." Upon getting them to the other side I motioned for the boy. "Help me with your sister." He seemed to undertand me this time for he reached up for her. Then I was able to reach back with my good arm and swing the girl down.

"Wait here for your mama." Then to the boy. "Watch over your little sisters."

"One more trip, Fred, then there's a little unfinished business."

Upon reaching the other shore I took my foot out of the stirrup. Speaking to the older girl, "Put your foot in." Then I said to her mother. "Give her a boost, my arm just ain't up to it."

With help from her mother the girl was settled down behind me. "Just hold on tight."

"I'll drive the horses across. You shouldn't have any trouble going afoot. Just go slow."

In just a few minutes all were situated on the other side walking up to the village with no name. Turning Fred, we rode back to Mal de Ojo. The north side of the village was fully ablaze. Dismounting, I rummaged through the saddlebags for the remaining three sticks of dynamite.

Mounting, I rode close to the fountain, where now the trees were on fire. "Ready to ride?" I asked Fred. I held the three sticks and leaned over to a burning ember, lit the three fuses, and put them in my left hand where I held the reins.

Throwing one into the market, I spurred Fred, "Yhaw!" and he took off. I took the second stick and threw it midway down the buildings. Spurring harder, I had to get rid of the last stick. I flung it to the walk at the end of the row of buildings. It hit, bounded once and then came the massive explosion from all three sticks.

Dirt, splinters, and debris flew up around us. Something hit Fred in the haunch and he started bucking. I grabbed the saddlehorn with my right hand as my left arm was now almost useless.

He finally settled down, and not too soon; I was fortunate to have held on. I looked at his right hip and he had a large splinter embedded. "Now don't you buck." I reached back and pulled it out. It was about two inches deep. When I was back in Texas, I'd clean it up.

I rode back where the market once was. Then I spied what I was looking for, a broken lamp. Two matches were left in my pocket. My eyes went to one of the bloodstones and with both matches in my hand I struck them across. They flared up and I made sure they were aflame, then flipped them on the split kerosene. There was a flash and the flame began to roll across the colllapsed and destroyed building. Soon the village of Mal de Ojo would be nothing but ashes.

"Let's go to Texas, Fred."

CHAPTER 35 – Aftermath

I rode up to the corral and Lorenzo was standing beside it. "Lorenzo, help me off." He came over to my side. As I swung my leg over I fell, knocking him down.

I awoke to stifling heat and darkness. My shoulder was burning like fire. It couldn't be, no...Hades? Then I saw the face of Ignacious and he gave me that wide smile.

"Where am I?" I asked no one in particular.

"The little village," replied Ignacious. "There was an empty jacal; it is now our private hospital."

I tried to get up, but felt woozy, so laid my head back down. "The Senora, she will be by, or the boy," said Ignacious.

"You were very weak, sleep long," he continued.

"How long?" I asked.

"Maybe day and a half, maybe more."

Sighing, I just laid there. Then asked, "Is Brown in here?"

"The other Gringo? Si, he is here, but very bad. He has not gained consciousness, and groans all the time. He is in much pain, I think."

"How 'bout you?"

"I probably live, maybe. Leg, it is very bad."

Since it was so dark, I didn't bother to look over at his leg. My hand moved up to touch my shoulder. It was bandaged tightly. Lorenzo's mother, most likely.

I figured I could try to get up one more time. Swinging my legs off my pallet I pushed with my right arm until I was sitting up. It was an effort, but I managed it. My head was swirling some.

"Senor," came Lorenzo's voice from the entrance. "You should not be up."

"Help me find my boots." He just stood there. "Don't be gawkin', I need my boots."

He went over to a little table by the entrance and picked up my boots that were sitting beside it and brought them to me. "I don't think...."

"Then don't, just help me."

I couldn't pull with my left hand so Lorenzo helped me stand. I pulled with my right hand and he reached to pull on the other side. He couldn't get at the correct angle to pull on the right boot. Being in front of me, when he tried to pull, his head bumped my stomach, knocking me back down on the pallet.

He started laughing, then stopped quickly thinking I might get mad. When I looked at him, I couldn't help it, I started laughing as well. We must have been comical, for even Ignacious was joining in the joviality. Lorenzo helped me back up. This time I reached and pulled on the left side, Lorenzo went to my side and pulled from there. Finally, success! The left boot was not so difficult to manage now that we had figured out how to get the job done.

"Help me over to the cantina," I said. There wasn't much he could do, but I could tell it made him feel good to be helpful. As we left the jacal I thought I could detect the smell of smoke in the air.

We had gone about half-way when out of the cantina burst Lorenzo's mother. She started in on him; I didn't know the words, but he was getting a scolding. Then she turned on me. "Senor, you shouldn't be up."

"Just goin' over to the cantina for some coffee."

We started again moving to the cantina with Lorenzo's mother walking behind us, barking every once in a while at Lorenzo. Entering the building, Lorenzo helped me sit down and the senora brought me some coffee.

"I'm also a mite hungry." That made her smile.

Lorenzo's father came over and sat with me. "I buried your friend," he said softly. "I will show you."

I looked at him and nodded. *"Gracias."*

"We," he motioned with his hand pointing all around the cantina, so I assumed he meant his family, "will take care of his grave."

I thought of Benito when the tortillas were set in front of me; reckon I always will. Filling one with beans I devoured it in seconds.

"The other Ranger should be back in a while with a wagon," said Lorenzo's father.

"Other Ranger? What other Ranger?" I asked.

"He came in right after you passed out. We have to get Ignacious and the unconscious one to a doctor in Laredo. They cannot be helped here."

I was still in the cantina eating, when I heard the sound of a wagon pulling in front. Pushing myself up from the table, I ambled to the doorway. There, climbing down from the wagon was Ty.

"Forgot all 'bout you. How's the shoulder? Figured you would have your feet propped up somewheres."

"Almost back to normal," he stopped and pointed at mine. "Heard you took a bullet."

"Benito's dead."

"When I didn't see him, and was told that a Ranger was buried, I thought it was probably him. How'd it happen?"

I waved a hand at him. "Not now, I'll tell you later."

That thought seem to exhaust me, then it hit me. I looked at Lorenzo's father. "The women and children, where are they?"

"They left," he said. "Only one family went back to Mexico. They have relatives down there somewhere. The others traveled north to find work; maybe in Del Rio."

I had thought that maybe Hector or Roberto would have stopped by to see me. "Don't be sad," said Lorenzo's father. "They did stop and wanted to thank you, but you were still asleep. They needed to travel together."

I started walking back to the jacal. "Need to lay down; tired," I told them. The truth was that Ty showing up asking about Benito and the sudden realization that those I saved were gone wore on my mind. I suddenly felt very weary.

CHAPTER 36

I slept fitfully, either from the pain in my shoulder or from the pain in my soul; I didn't know which. I finally struggled out of bed, pulling my boots on by myself this time. Walking outside, I saw the wagon loaded with hay ready to transport the wounded.

They carried Tom out first. His arm was bound to his side, and it looked like he was wearing a large mitten to keep his thumb, or where he thumb used to be, from being banged around. He was very pale, just about the color of fresh milk, and still had not opened his eyes. Gently, they laid him in the hay and then cushioned him with it.

After they had him settled, they went back for Ignacious. This was the first time I got a glimpse of his leg. It was swollen to twice its normal size. The senora had wrapped it loosely, so I couldn't actually see where the snake had left the mark of its fangs. He was laid beside Tom, but since he could sit up, Tom's saddle was placed behind him.

"You're next, Elias," said Ty.

"Oh, no, I'm ridin'."

"Senor, you are not able," said Lorenzo's father.

Ignoring him, I hollered, "Lorenzo! Saddle Fred for me!" Then I looked back at Ty and the father. "If I can sit in a wagon, I can sit on my saddle."

In a few minutes, Lorenzo had my horse ready, along with all my gear. Fumbling through my saddlebags I found my little hide-away pouch. Opening it, I took out an item.

Handing the item to Lorenzo, he exclaimed. "A silver dollar! A whole dollar!"

"For taking care of Fred and helping me," I paused and then sighed, "And my friend."

I checked the cinch, then made sure everything was tied down tight; Lorenzo had done a good job. Not being able to use the stirrup to mount I stepped up on the rails of the corral. After I settled myself down in the saddle, I rode to the wagon where Ty was sitting. "Go on along, I'll catch you in a little while."

Ty nodded, and with a flick of the reins the horses began to pull the wagon down the road toward Laredo.

Going back to Lorenzo, I said, "Show me where my friend is buried."

He took me to a spot, back behind the cantina a ways where there were a few other graves. Off to the side, near a mesquite tree was the grave of my friend; no, my brother. There was a small, rudiment of a cross driven into the ground.

"My papa said your friend would like the shade of the tree," Lorenzo said solemnly.

I nodded, "He was right."

The sorrow, the anger; it was all gone now. There was nothing to feel. I grasped for some feeling, but it was just emptiness; a hollow feeling deep inside.

Turning Fred, we walked out of the little graveyard. I put my hand up in a half-hearted wave to Lorenzo, but didn't look back. Fred just kept walking, sensing that there was no need to hurry.

Half-hour, hour later, I don't really know, we caught up with the wagon. The road was seldom used and therefore very rough. Ty didn't want to bang the two injured passengers around any more than he had to so he moved slowly. I didn't relish the idea, but reckoned it would take at least two days, more likely three days, to reach Laredo.

Ty had to do most of the work. There wasn't much he could do for Tom. Throughout the day Ignacious would dribble water into his mouth, but that was about all that could be done. It was probably for the best that he was not conscious; I could only imagine the pain he would feel.

Ignacious, on the other hand, had to have his bandages changed. There was no fever, so that was good, but by the end of the second day there was a distinct odor. On the third day, he laid back and started to moan.

Upon entering Laredo, we immediatley inquired of a doctor. Ty drove the wagon to the doctor's door and went inside. I stayed mounted as it was an ordeal for me to mount and dismount. Within seconds the doctor and Ty came out and they were able to get Ignacious inside.

They came back out with a litter and yelling at a couple of men, who were just sitting around biding their time, to help load Tom up and carry him inside.

Seconds later, the doctor came back out and pointed at me. "You! Get down and in here!"

"Me?" I asked, pointing at myself.

"You! Get off that horse and in my office. Now!" he was as bossy as an old woman.

This was the first time I'd tried dismouting by myself. Ty had always been there to help. I rode to the wagon, and stepped off Fred to the bed of the wagon. Putting my good arm on the edge of the wagon I sat down, then scooted off the edge. Looking around sheepishly I was sure glad no one was there to note my dismounting procedure.

Upon entering the building I noticed four beds; two now occupied by our patients. "Take off that dirty shirt," the doctor ordered.

"Um, doc, I don't think I can do it by myself," I said.

He came over with a pair of scissors. "It's my only shirt!" I exclaimed, holding on to it.

"Has to come off, and by the looks of it, there's only half a shirt there."

After cutting the bandages and the shirt off he began to clean my wounds. He was not of the most genteel manner and started the wound bleeding. Then he began in earnest: prob, scrub, bathe in hot water, then do it again.

"Front looks pretty good, but take a grip on the edge of the table. "This will hurt some."

Hurt! The pain went all the way down to my toes, and back up.

"Sorry, but I had to do some cutting. There was some bad stuff there." Then he began the process as before of scrubbing and bathing the wound. "Hang on again, I'm going to put some disinfectant on your wounds. It might burn just a little."

Glad he said, "just a little." Whooee! I couldn't imagine the feeling if he had said "a lot."

After bandaging me up, he pointed to a small trunk. "Rummage through it. There's probably a shirt that will fit you. There might be a hole or two in them, but they are clean."

"You there," he pointed at Ty. "Help me with the Mexican."

I started to walk out when the doc spoke again. "See

me in a couple of days. Charge for services rendered is $1.00, just place it on the desk."

I looked at Ty. He pulled a little bag out of his vest pocket and gave me the money.

Smiling, I reached and took it and placed $1.00 Texas Ranger script on the desk. "Here," and then to Ty. "I'll be at the livery."

CHAPTER 37 – Resignation

I had been loafing around town, not able to do much with one arm. However, each day I could feel my left arm getting stronger. Sometime each day I went over to the doctor's office to check on Tom. On the second day he replaced my bandages, and scrubbed me with some of that burning disinfectant again.

Tom still hadn't regained consciousness. The doctor said that his injury was beyond his expertise. He didn't remove the rawhide for fear of exposing the artery.

"There's a little infection, but he doesn't have a fever," he told Ty and me. "Right now, we just wait and see."

"Gringo," came the voice of Ignacious as I was getting up to leave. "For saving my life, I thank you. I even get to keep my leg although the doctor had to gouge out much of the rotten flesh."

I looked at him, and then nodded and went out. He was the type that would survive, mostly at the expense of other people.

It was the fourth day since our arrival in Laredo. I was

in the livery helping put hay in the troughs to feed the horses boarded there, when Ty came in to give me some information.

"The Captain's in town. He's in an office at the hotel," he said and started to leave. "Oh yeah, Tom has gained consciousness."

Putting down the pitchfork I wandered down to the hotel. The door to McNelly's office was open and I could see him sitting there behind a desk. He was talking to Armstrong who was sitting across from him.

I went to the door and entered. Armstrong was getting up to bar my entrance until he could find out my business.

"Sit back down, John. Come on in, Elias." The Captain stood up to shake my hand. "Have a seat."

I stood there, with my head slightly bowed, not wanting to sit. "Captain...."

"I heard of your daring escapades in Mal de Ojo," he said, then sincerely added. "I'm truly sorry about Benito, and Corporal Brown too."

"Captain," I started again. "Meaning no disrespect to you, but I quit." Taking the badge I had been holding in my hand, I placed it on the table. "I'm not cut out to be a Ranger, or lawman of any sort."

"Why, Butler, I hear you did a magnificent job of cleaning out that nest of vipers," said Armstrong.

My head jerked up at the mention of "vipers." "Yeah, I got rid of them all right, and only God knows how many more."

"Elias, I would really like for you to reconsider and stay in the Rangers. We're not quite rid of Cortinas yet, though we've made great headway. You've taken care of this El Diablo, and the savagery he was loosing on the people of Texas."

He paused and looked at me. "Elias, sometimes the work of an officer of the law is hard. Remember, that God most often uses men to see justice accomplished on this earth. If it were not for men like you and Benito, wickedness would prevail. Men like this El Diablo, would run rampant and ravage the people.

"Sorry, Captain," I replied. "The Lord says, 'vengeance is Mine,' but after all I saw happenin', vengeance became mine! I wasn't showin' justice, I just wanted revenge."

"Elias...."

"Captain, you don't understand. I had to put a bullet through Benito's head. He was closer than a brother to me. After that I didn't care who suffered, I just wanted to destroy," I paused then added. "And I did!"

"There's no need to punish yourself. Texas needs you; the Rangers need men like you to clean up this rotten evil, so that honest, God-fearing folk can live in peace and security."

"Sorry, Captain. I have one more job left to do; get Tom Brown back to his wife as I promised." I nodded at Armstrong and walked out.

I didn't know it at the time, but right after I left the office Captain McNelly asked Armstrong. "Where's Miles Forrest?"

"Brownsville."

"Get him up here, immediatly."

I waited around town for a couple more days helping out at the livery. They even paid me by not charging me for Fred. It was time for me to get Tom.

"Can he travel, Doc?" I asked.

"Carefully, it would be best in a wagon. He can't use his hand. It would probably be for the best as I can't do anything more for him. There are doctors in San Antonio or Austin that may be able to help him more."

"Let's go," I said to Tom. "Time for you to get back to Sarah and that unborn son."

"No way! I'm not going back, half a man!" he yelled.

"You've always been half a man from what I've seen."

He started to rant. That loosed something in me and I hauled off and punched him, knocking him off the chair in which he was sitting.

"Now, see here!" cried the doctor. "You can't...."

"Can't? You just watch, Doc," I said and reached down to pull Tom off the floor, ready to slug him again.

"I promised Sarah I'd bring you back to her. What you do after I drop your no-good self off is your business. Reckon it would be best for her if you did pack up and leave."

He was whimpering now like a beat pup. "I can't even work, with this," and he held up his bandaged hand.

"Be a man, for once, Tom Brown! Learn to get by! You still have one good hand the Lord left you with. Ifn you've a mind to, you can be a better man with one hand than you ever were with two."

I looked at the doc. "Get him ready to go. I'll be back in an hour with a wagon."

Within the hour, I had a wagon all loaded with supplies at the doctor's office. Tom came out and I could see there was some pain etched on his face. He and the doctor walked to the back of the wagon.

"What are you doin'?" I asked. "Get up here on the seat."

They looked at me, but listened. The doctor helped Tom climb aboard, and I noticed he left room for me to sit down.

"Here," and I handed him the reins and walked over to mount Fred. "You might as well start usin' that left hand now."

EPILOGUE

I heaved a sigh as I finished putting together the story. My heart was beating heavily as I thought of what my great grandfather must have faced and the feelings he felt.

It took some time to piece together this portion of his life, but now I understood the heading of the article, "Evil...Ashes." It was the destruction of Mal de Ojo, when Elias Butler burnt it to the ground.

Now, more than ever, I couldn't sell the place. I needed to get a lawyer to draw up some kind of contract that would satisfy Will and especially Betsy. If they would just settle for a down payment I was sure we could sell our house and pay them off. I was very fortunate my wife was understanding and going along with me on this venture.

Taking a sip of coffee, a thought struck me. I rushed over and opened the trunk and began to rummage through it. There, where I found the guns and badges, was a piece of cloth. Slowly, with anticipation, I began to unwrap the cloth. There it was—a bloodstone, red with specks and streaks of darker red within it.

But, I wondered, where was the other stone? I went back to the pages of papers and journals that I had sitting on the table. In these, there must be a clue. Maybe it was just lost, because it didn't make sense for my great grandfather to keep one stone but not the other.

Also, in the midst of all that paper was more insight into the life of my great grandfather, Elias Butler. I had found several badges, so he must have gone back into the work of law enforcement. I almost laughed out loud; I thought that maybe I inherited my fear of snakes from him.

NOTES

Evil Eye:
The term *evil eye* is used specifically four times in the King James Version of the Bible and alluded to several more times.

Jesus, in Mark, chapter 7, speaks of those things that defile a man, things that proceed out of him. In verse 22, He specifically mentions "an evil eye."

Most of the time when it is referred to it is speaking of a malevolent or sensuous glare. It may often cause misfortune to the person upon whom it is placed. Many believed that the person with the *evil eye* was able to cast a spell on others.

Bloodstone:
There are many beliefs concerning the power of the bloodstone, from stopping the *evil eye* to healing qualities and giving the qualities of courage and strength.

From the time of the Roman Republic forward the legend said that it was formed when the blood of Jesus fell on jasper and it was stained at the foot of the Cross.

It was often placed in an amulet to protect against the

evil eye and other forms of sickness and magical spells.
One other interesting facet of the bloodstone was that is was known as a symbol of justice.

Leander McNelly:
Captain McNelly was instrumental in the forming of the new Texas Rangers after Reconstruction. He died of tuberculosis at the age of 33. Death occurred on September 4, 1877 in Burton, Texas.
By the way, McNelly arrested King Fisher, but Fisher was released shortly after.

Badges of the Texas Rangers:
Texas Ranger's badges were not issued until 1887. It was used in this book for effect. However, Rangers could have their own badges made before that date.

ABOUT THE AUTHOR

Donald C. Adkisson was born and raised in Boulder, Colorado. He met his wife, Annie Baker, while attending Evangel University in Springfield, Missouri. Following six years of service in the U.S. Air Force he began his career in education. He earned his Master's degree from Northern Kentucky University.

After being involved in education for thirty-nine years as a teacher, coach and administrator he recently retired, and moved from San Antonio, Texas where he spent twenty-two years at a Christian school. Currently he lives in Cleveland, Texas and is planning on building a home in Coldspring, Texas to concentrate more on his writing.

Since 2001, he has written a daily devotion. He has recently changed its name from the "Daily Paine" to "Echoes From the Campfire." He is the author of one novel, the prequel to this one, titled, *The True and Unbiased Life of Elias Butler.* He also has published a devotional book titled, *Trails in the Wilderness.*

He has been married to Annie for forty-six years. They like to travel this vast, wonderful country. He enjoys traveling to places so he can get a "feel" of what it might have been like for those people who went there before us. They have two daughters and four grandchildren. He would tell you that you can't get the mountains out of his blood, but there is certainly no place like Texas.

Currently, he is in the process of developing a facebook page: Ira Paine....Just Talkin'. There is also a website containing the daily devotions: irapaine.com.

D.C. Adkisson

34246484R00096

Made in the USA
Columbia, SC
14 November 2018